WAGON BUDDY

STEVE STRED

WAGON BUDDY

The light shone brightly on my face, the chair uncomfortable, and the two Detectives' glares burrowing into my face.

I sucked deeply on my cigarette. I was surprised they had allowed me this request. They had denied me a beer, but they said alright to a cigarette, probably to humour me, knowing there was no chance they would believe my story.

"Look Scott, just tell us again, but keep the imaginary friend out of it. How did you kill them, and where did you put the bodies? We have the footage of you pulling the wagon. We can see the girl's body in the back of the wagon, and like we told your lawyer, it makes no sense to us how there's no trace of you on the girl at all. But we know you did it. Spill the beans."

I just smirked. Ever since I was 6 years old, none of

this made any sense, and now I was supposed to magically make them understand?

"Listen, I already told you. There's nothing else I can say. I didn't do it, I never killed any of them, I don't know where they are, or where it put them. I always assumed it ate them, but it doesn't exist, right?"

The larger detective slammed the desk so hard it made me jump. He stood up and left the room. The other detective just sat and stared, frustrated by my persistence, but trying to find a way to get me to confess. Again I smirked. He could try as hard as he wanted, but it wasn't going to happen. I had nothing to confess to, at the end of the day, I was purely an accomplice, but I had to tread carefully here to make sure I didn't spend my life in jail.

"Ok, you want me to tell the story again?" I offered up, not sure what to do here, knowing that my lawyer wasn't coming for some time, and that they wouldn't let me leave.

"That's the problem Scott, IT'S A STORY! WE WANT THE TRUTH!" he yelled, now also slamming his folder down, spilling its contents onto the table between us. He quickly tried to put everything back into the folder, but I was able to see the pictures they had, photos pulled from the dash cam video. My eyes went wide at one photo. In every other photo I was alone, pulling my little red wagon behind me, that horrible lady's body lying in the wagon, clearly dead. But in one photo, there was a third individual. My wagon buddy. The figure was blurry and out of focus, but I could make out all of the details of my imaginary friend.

"Do you see that, right there?" I asked the man, who was now sitting in his chair, legs splayed out, elbows resting on his thighs, hands supporting his lowered head.

He slowly looked up, checking to see what I was alluding too.

"Scott," he said slowly, pulling the photo around so we could both look at it together.

"You are not supposed to see this. This was supposed to be privileged for your lawyer. We cannot discuss this photo without your lawyer present."

"I don't care, look right here, that is the murderer, that's who has been killing the people. That's my wagon buddy."

I was getting more and more anxious, not understanding why they wouldn't believe me, and trying hard to show them who was really responsible.

"Ok, Scott, tell me again, tell me about this wagon buddy of yours, but if your lawyer shows up, we stop. Fair?"

I nodded my head yes.

"Ok, let me turn the recorder on again." He pushed the record button making it official.

"This is Detective Dave Linear, officially recording Scott Carlsville, of his account of the missing people here in our city. Scott, you may begin. If you need to stop, please say stop and I will turn off the device. If you need a drink at any time, please also let me know."

He motioned for me to start, and I cleared my throat.

"Hi, hello, uhhh, hello, this is Scott. Um, ok, where to start. Ok, when I was 6 years old my mother and father separated. My father was a jerk and left my mother for my babysitter. My mother didn't do so well and started to drink. It was around this time I wanted someone I could talk to, being an only child, so one day my friend showed up, and things got better for me, for a short period of time."

Detective Linear rolled his eyes at this, but I didn't care, I was telling the truth. So I continued.

I was an only child and my parents didn't socialize much, so I was on my own a lot. I craved companionship, and we never had any pets, so I developed an imaginary friend, who quickly became as real to me as I am too you. He showed up about a week after my father left. They had a fight. I didn't pay attention to it, I was just sitting in the living room coloring or whatever, and they were yelling. The yelling was getting louder and louder, my mother really shouting, before I realized everything had gone completely silent. Then my father stormed by, carrying a suitcase, and as he walked out the door, he looked back, making eye contact. I never saw or heard from him again.

My mother began drinking almost immediately, cursing my father, cursing my babysitter, cursing everything. I tried to cheer her up, acting silly, drawing her pictures, but after I showed her how I could jump off the kitchen table and land on the couch in the living room, she beat me good and hard. Spanked my bum, punched my sides, I think she just let loose on me with some of her pent up anger.

I ran outside crying, running into the back yard, and tripped over my wagon. I guess I forgot to put it away, or some other power had moved it in my way, you know how life works, right? Well, I turned and looked and the wagon brought a smile to my face instantly. I loved that wagon, and maybe it was the memories of my father pulling me around in it, but I got up, grabbed the handle and began pulling it behind me around the yard. It was about the third or fourth go a-round when it suddenly got heavier, and I heard a thump, as though someone or something had jumped in behind me, onto the wagon.

Turning, I was shocked to see a figure sitting in my wagon.

A friend!

"Hello, who are you?" I asked excitedly, glad to not be alone, hopeful we could become best friends.

The figure stepped out of the wagon, standing before me. They wore a long dark cloak, covering their entire body, and a frightening mask on their face. The mouth was pulled back in a large leering smile, the eyes cut out, showing cold black pupils behind it. The person, or thing, had long black hair, hanging out from behind the mask.

When they stood up, I became frightened. This was a tall scary figure, a dark atmosphere surrounding them, and me being only 6, I knew then that something wasn't right. The figure, seeing my small frame, knelt down to my eye level, and the mask shifted slightly.

What I saw behind the mask has stayed with me to this day, and has at times given me nightmares and caused me to wake up screaming.

The skin below was decayed and falling from the bone. The gristle appeared to have white makeup all over, covering the tissue, but it couldn't hide the cuts, scars and missing flesh. Maggots were crawling around in the open wounds, fighting over each other for morsels of nourishment.

"Hello Scott," the creature said, its voice deep and tasting like dirt.

My soul shrunk as it spoke, knowing that this thing was no friend of mine, but I would have no choice in the matter. Even at 6 years old, I knew it had chosen me.

"Hello," I meekly replied, wishing it would stand up again, its breath making me nauseous.

"Scott, I am here to be your friend. You are lonely, and I am a friend. From time to time I may ask you for a favour, but I am here for you. Would you like to play?"

I nodded my head yes, of course I would like to play. I was so sad and so lonely.

"Great! How about I pull you for a bit in the wagon?"

I eagerly jumped in the wagon, excited to have a friend.

"Mister, what should I call you?"

"Scott, you wouldn't like my real name. So how about you just call me your wagon buddy?"

Wagon buddy. That sounded just great.

With that we were off, and the giant figure, cloaked in all black, wearing a frightening mask to cover its decaying face, pulled me around and around the yard.

When my mother finally called me to come in for dinner, she kept asking why I was smiling so much.

"My new friend played with me! I have never had a friend like this!"

All through dinner, my mother kept looking over at me. I felt like she wanted to apologize for having hit me so many times, but I appeared fine, and I think she just wanted to put that transgression behind her and move on from it. After dinner, I ran back outside to play with my wagon buddy, but I couldn't find them anywhere. I dejectedly put the wagon back by the side of the house and went back in. I hoped they would come back soon.

A few days went by before they returned.

I had been dragging my feet around, driving my mother crazy with my sadness, when she finally exploded and threw her cup at me. I ran outside, fleeing her antics and aggression, and raced to the backyard.

I was so focused on getting away from her that I didn't see my wagon buddy standing there, and ran directly into its body. It felt like I ran into a tree with a hundred short branches. Later in life, when thinking back about that incident, I realized that I had connected directly with its skeleton.

I let out a noise and fell back to the ground in pain.

The figure didn't flinch, never giving up any ground at all.

"Hey!" I complained from below, trying to make it known that it was the figure's fault I ran into it.

"Scott, you need to be more observant. Sometimes it's the little things we see that fill in the pieces of the bigger puzzle."

I had no idea what that meant, or what it was trying to say. I didn't care, my body was still in pain from the impact. Before I stood up though, my new companion was already improving my mood.

"You want to play again? I can pull you in the wagon?"

My face lit up, smiling wide, excited to have my friend again.

"Oh yes please!" I said, jumping up, grabbing the wagon from the house and throwing myself into the back, suddenly pain free and full of energy.

"Here we go!" the thing yelled, and began to pull me behind it, running faster and faster. The wind picked up as it ran, blowing my hair back. In that moment, I don't think I have ever smiled as wide as I did then.

When I think back on those times now, I always remember it in slow motion, the cloak flapping, the mask bouncing, but not enough to let me see the horrors behind. I would be gripping the wagon tight, body jostled around in the back, as the wagon careened and sped around our yard. The creature would zig and zag around my old swing set, and then dart around the trees that had been planted but ultimately left to die.

Those were some of the greatest moments of my life. Frankly, I wish those times had never stopped, that I had never grown older. Once I got older, the creature took advantage of me.

My wagon buddy visited me on and off for several more years like clockwork. I knew that it would go away for a few days, but then would return and we would play. As I grew and got bigger, I also began to take turns pulling the creature. While exhausting, it was exhilarating to be truly playing with my friend.

Finally though, things went off the rails.

On a normal day, my wagon buddy came by, and we played, taking turns pulling each other around the yard. It was a Sunday, and I was a bit saddened that I would be returning to school tomorrow. Two kids had started to bully me repeatedly, and it made the days long and hard.

"Scott, tomorrow, I need you to bring your wagon with you to school."

"Why? The kids will bully me even more. Probably call me a baby even. I'm sick of being pushed, kicked or worse."

"Don't worry about them. Let them call you names. After school though, tell the big kid you want to speak to his father. Then bring your wagon and wait behind the school."

"You mean Ryan?"

"Yes, Ryan, the big one. Tell him you want to speak to his father. Swear at him if you must. Just bring him to the back, and make sure you bring your wagon."

I didn't sleep well that night, but when I woke up, I found I was excited to go to school. I asked my mother if I could bring my wagon, just to make sure, and she said that was fine. Arriving at school, though, made my excitement turn to panic.

Just as I had predicted, I was teased mercilessly at school that day, for bringing my wagon, for having no friends, for having no father. But I didn't care, not then, because my wagon buddy had told me not to worry about it.

As lunch ended, I found Ryan in the hallway. Even though he was a good four inches taller than me, and close to twenty pounds heavier, I walked up to him and shoved him as hard as I could, causing him to slam into his locker.

"What the hell, loser?" he squawked.

"After school, I need to speak to your father. Tell him to meet me around back, I will be waiting with my wagon."

I just turned and walked away, worried that he was going to punch me from behind.

School ended, and I quickly went and got my wagon, and went around to the back of the school, and waited. And waited. And waited some more. I was convinced that Ryan's father wasn't going to show up.

Finally I heard someone walking, and a man came around the corner. He was larger, but looked like an older version of my bully. Ryan was with him, but as they approached, the man made Ryan stay back.

"What's the meaning of this? My son Ryan says you pushed him today?"

I looked around, hoping to see my wagon buddy, worried when I didn't.

"Sir, sir, your son has been bullying me for some time. Calling me names, making fun of my father leaving us. It needs to stop."

The man looked back at his son, calling out to him.

"Ryan, this true? You bullying this kid?"

Ryan looked down, slowly nodding his head.

The man looked back at me, and then he proceeded to laugh.

"You the kid he has told me about?" he said, laughing heartedly. "The one with no friends and no father. Left your mother for the babysitter. Don't blame him, having a useless son. Come on Ryan, let's go."

He turned and started to walk away, when I noticed

my wagon slowly start rolling. Faster and faster it rolled after the man, before striking the back of his legs and knocking him down.

"Hey? What the hell?"

I felt the air beside me bristle, as something rushed passed me in a hurry. Then I saw my wagon buddy standing over Ryan's father. Ryan saw it, turned and took off running. Ryan's father was paralyzed with fear, staring up at the large cloaked creature, the mask staring down at him.

"What are you?"

Those were the last words he spoke, as the creature, in the blink of an eye, removed its mask, and pounced on the man.

From where I stood, all I could hear was sucking and slurping sounds. The man didn't scream, didn't kick, he didn't make any noise. He just stayed on the ground, covered by my friend.

When my wagon buddy was finished, it stood up, turned and motioned for me to come over. I walked very slowly, scared for my life.

"Come Scott, but not too close, I don't want you to see the man. Hold the wagon steady, while I load the body onto it. Come now, quickly."

I grabbed the handle, holding tight, and waited for the sickening thud of the man's body, as the creature dropped it into the wagon.

"Now follow me please," it said, and it started to walk towards the ravine, and I followed.

When we got to the ravine behind the school, it stopped.

"Now turn away Scott, you don't want to see this. Once I take the body out, you can go home. You will sleep just fine, I promise, and you won't be bullied at this school anymore."

I felt the weight of the body leave the wagon, and I turned and ran as fast as I could. I didn't want to know what was happening, nor did I care, I just wanted to get home.

When I ran into the house, my lungs were on fire, hurting so badly I thought I would die.

"You are home late tonight Scott, is everything ok?"

I hadn't even noticed my mother sitting on the couch. Her voice startled me.

Catching my breath, I held up a finger to let her know I needed a second. I went and quickly got a glass of water, needing to drown my burning lungs.

"Sorry mother, yes everything is ok, I just had to stay late. I should have called or let you know earlier."

"That's ok, just glad you are home," she said, cracking open another can of beer.

"Dinner is ready, your plate is in the oven, help yourself, I am going to sit here and watch some television. If you want to discuss your day with me, please wait until my show is over."

I ate quickly before telling her I had homework, and retired to my room.

My wagon buddy was correct. I slept just fine that night, and while the creature came and visited every few days, I wasn't asked any favours for some time. And the figure had told me the truth as well, about being bullied. I wasn't bullied for the rest of my time at that school. It didn't happen again until high school, which is where I will pick up my story now.

The detective stood up abruptly, staring at me hard.

"Everything you say is a fantastical lie! I can't rightly believe that this is what happened! You sit here and tell me that Mr. Thompson, who has been missing for over 20 years now, was killed and consumed by a "creature"? I need a minute."

He left the room, slamming the door behind him.

I strained to grab my cup of water, the handcuffs biting into my wrists. When the detective had slammed the table, my cup had moved just enough that I wasn't able to get it. Maybe if I had all the fingers on my right hand, I would have been able to, but missing my thumb and index finger, made it impossible to reach.

The door flew open again, and this time both of the men returned.

"Can you please pass me my cup of water?" I asked, half expecting it to be denied.

The other detective moved it over to me, but didn't appear too happy to do so.

"Thank you," I said before talking a long gulp.

"Ok Scott, continue. I needed to get my partner here to be present to hear this, as there is only so much I can take of this farce on my own."

I nodded. I would continue, but not a single word I was speaking was a lie.

A few years went by in a blur, my wagon buddy coming and visiting, but as I got older, we stopped playing on the wagon for hours, and instead, the creature adapted to my changing interests.

My mother was still drinking, but managed to keep a steady job, and, I suspect, feeling bad at my father abandoning me, tried to overcompensate with gifts. The one gift she got me though, that I truly treasured, was a basketball backboard and hoop, which she had installed during the day while I was at school. That night when I came home, I was so surprised, I ran up and hugged her, not realizing it was the first time we had hugged in close to five years.

"Thank you, thank you, thank you," I kept saying, overjoyed that I would be able to play in the backyard whenever I wanted. The start of high school had been tough. New kids, new bullies, same old teasing. I didn't have a father, I had no friends, and I wasn't athletic. But I was tall. And so far in physical education, I had started to become a force in basketball. I was a good six inches taller than a lot of the kids in my grade, thanks to a growth spurt over the summer, which gave me a very obvious advantage while playing.

Funny thing was, as I got taller, so did my wagon buddy.

As for basketball, I was getting good enough to have the coach from the senior boys team ask me to come and try out. I did fairly well, and told my mother all about it that night over dinner.

I didn't make the team, but that was ok, I had a goal. I was in grade 9 and if I improved my playing skills, in grade 10 there was a good chance I could make the grade 11 and 12 team.

Seeing this basketball hoop in my own backyard was the best gift ever, and it surprised me to know my mother had been paying attention to what I was saying, not just drowning herself in her alcohol.

I ate dinner rapidly that night, and once I put my dishes away, excitedly asked if I was allowed to go out and play on the hoop.

"Of course, just make sure you come back in with enough time to do your homework."

I leapt out of the house and ran to the hoop. My mother had even purchased a brand new Spalding basketball for me, and the pebbles on the surface felt fantastic on my palms.

I decided that if I was going to improve, I needed to have structure for my time at home at the hoop. Much like practices at school, I couldn't just come and chuck the ball all night. I needed to work on drills and my hand-eye coordination. So I started by dribbling with one hand then focused on dribbling with the other. I also worked on walking with the ball and running while dribbling. Then I would cross over, and dribble between my legs. Finally I would do layups and then free throws. I felt so accomplished.

As the day became night, darkness creeping in, I decided to head back inside. As I walked towards the front of the house, I noticed my wagon sitting there, and decided to put the basketball in it.

Sometime in the middle of the night I was wrestled from my sleep by the sounds of the basketball being bounced in the back yard. Thinking someone was stealing my new gift, I rushed to my window, sliding it open, and looked out into the yard.

There I saw my wagon buddy, dribbling the ball, taking shots and appearing to be having a good time.

The creature stopped at one point, turned to look up at me, and then waved.

I returned the wave, and went back to bed, happy that my wagon buddy was excited by my new gift as well.

Over the next few days, school was particularly rough. A few of my new grade 12 bullies made it a point to body check me in the hallways, and one even made the effort to kick me in the groin when I was laying on the floor. All the other students laughed, not caring that I had been hurt.

When the weekend finally came, I was really glad. Two days away was always nice, and I couldn't wait to spend some quality time with my basketball.

Bad news greeted me when I got home though.

During the day, a landscaping company had accidentally cut down a tree, and it had fallen and landed in our backyard. They wouldn't be able to remove in until Monday, so that meant no basketball in the backyard.

After seeing my reaction, my mother decided I needed some cheering up.

"How about this Scotty, how about tomorrow

morning, you pack your ball and some water, I pack a small lunch and we will go to a basketball court somewhere here in the city, and I will read while you practice?"

I hugged her again, so excited.

"Yes, please, yes! Thank you!"

I vibrated for the rest of the night. I craved for my mother to spend time with me, not with her drinks, and this meant we would actually spend time together and she would watch me, seeing how good I had become.

The next day, we got ready and got in the car. My mother suggested we go a few blocks over to a park that had a basketball court.

It only took ten minutes to arrive, but I was in heaven, sitting in the passenger seat, my mother driving. We were doing something together, and I couldn't have been any happier.

Arriving and parking, we made our way over to the court, and she laid out a blanket she had packed and took out her book. I was the first person to arrive at the court, so I was able to choose the basket closest to where she was laying.

I followed my routine, warming up, then doing some drills, before starting to do some free throws. After hitting five throws in a row, I heard some clapping, and looking over, saw my mother was standing near the edge of the court, cheering me on.

"Way to go Scott, I didn't know you were so good! It looks like that basketball hoop in the backyard is paying off!"

"Thanks, it sure is!"

I got back to it, and hit five more in a row. On the 11th attempt overall, the ball hit the rim just off to the side and bounced away. I turned to chase after it, and in doing so, spotted my grade 11 and 12 tormentors entering the court. One of them scooped up my ball, holding it as they walked towards me.

"Hey loser, who said you could play at our court?"

It was Gary. He was the best basketball player in our school, and also the biggest bully.

"May I have my ball back please?" I asked calmly, not wanting to engage with them, especially with my mother sitting court side.

"Where is your father? He decide to stay away like always?"

I motioned with my hands for them to toss my ball back, but knew they wouldn't be obliging that easily.

"Come and take your ball if you want it."

I felt like a big shot in front of my mother, so I took a step towards them, wanting to grab my ball, when the kid holding the ball wound up and threw it at my face as hard as he could. I didn't have time to react, other than feeling the impact of the hard rubber slamming into my nose, immediately snapping my head back, causing me to drop to the court.

My nose started bleeding, pain blowing up all over my face, and while I tried to reach up to it and apply some pressure, Gary walked over and punched me as hard as he could.

I saw stars and felt dizzy. I could hear my mother screaming for them to stop, from off in the distance, but the ringing in my ears muffled her voice.

Unfortunately for me, they weren't done, and once again I was slammed in the face with the ball, before I felt them begin kicking me.

My mother arrived, begging them to leave me alone, and I heard another older male jog over and yell at the kids to stop.

"You are lucky they saved you this time scum," the boys yelled as they ran away.

I faded in and out of consciousness for the next little bit, but from what I could remember, the man who came over helped my mother get me to the car, and she took me to the hospital.

The results weren't great. Broken nose, broken teeth and a broken rib. To make matters worse, I had to wear a plastic face shield, protecting my face from being bumped or hit while my nose healed up.

Even worse than the face mask though, was that I

wouldn't be able to participate in any activities for about a month or longer, depending on how my rib healed.

I was crushed. I wouldn't even be able to use the basketball hoop in the backyard at all. The Doctor was pretty stern, saying if I didn't rest, surgery might be required.

My mother tried to comfort me, make me feel better, trying to joke with me on the ride home, but I wasn't having any of it. I just wasn't in the mood.

When we pulled into the driver my mother turned off the car and then we sat quietly.

"Scotty," she began, in a half whisper, "I'm sorry you get made fun of and teased. Please know I would have preferred for your father to not have left. I heard what they were saying to you. Would you like me to home school you? Or look at a different school for you to go to?"

My mother had never said anything to me before about my father. She also had never really verbally acknowledged my bullying. But I guess her having witnessed it first hand, and having seen the damage from my beating, she felt partially responsible.

"No, that's ok," I slurred, my face still swollen, my mouth not totally used to the way the plastic mask felt.

I got out of the car and began to walk into the house, when my mother called my name.

Turning, she bounced my basketball to me.

I gingerly grabbed it, trying not to let my rib area ache.

"I made sure we grabbed your ball," she said before turning away, tears in her eyes.

It was tough for me to sleep that night. I couldn't get comfortable, and I was broken and bruised. Finally I drifted off, but it didn't last long before I heard the distinct sound of a basketball being bounced outside. Looking out the window, there was my wagon buddy, playing some hoops.

I put on my mask, and headed down, making sure not to disturb my mother, who had passed out on the couch, empty cans laying around her, and went out to the backyard.

"Nice mask," the creature said when I approached.

"Not funny. Sorry I can't play, broken rib," I said, pointing towards the area.

"I know. Don't worry."

The creature bounced the ball to me, then turned and disappeared into the darkness, leaving me all alone.

I was on pins and needles when I finally returned to school. My nerves caused me to throw up that morning, two weeks later, which hurt like nobody's business. My ribs hadn't fully healed yet.

I was still wearing my face mask, and to say I was self-conscious would be a gross understatement.

When I entered the school I could feel everyone's eyes looking at me, but I knew the only way through was to walk with my head held high. The truth was, I was worried if I lowered my eyes, the older kids would blindside me with a body check, or worse.

Thankfully I was able to make it to my locker without any surprise violence.

I didn't have any real friends, but the kid beside my locker would talk to me once in a while. He saw me approaching, staring at my mask. When I opened my locker up, he kept staring, until finally he spoke.

"Thought you were dead. Your face is awful."

Then he turned and walked away.

The day went by relatively quickly, and with 30 minutes left in my last class, I was getting excited to leave and go home. Sitting near the windows, movement outside alerted my attention.

There, at the end of the school running track, in the playground, swinging on the swings, was my wagon buddy. Every time the creature pumped its legs, the long black cloak it wore floated behind it.

I felt a lump in my throat. This wasn't a good sign. Staring at the thing, as it swung higher and higher, I didn't know what to do. Then it waved at me, happily enjoying its play time, glad to see me in the school. It was like a younger sibling spotting their older sibling through a chain link fence.

I stopped staring and turned back to the teacher, trying to ignore the swinging distraction.

When the final bell rang, I looked back nervously, but was glad to see the swings sitting empty.

I quickly went to my locker, putting my books away, and grabbed my backpack. I was starting to think I would be home-free, not picked on or bullied at all that first day back, but alas, it was not to be.

As I turned to leave, closing my locker, my attackers returned, walking down the hallway, staring at me angrily.

"Hey loser, do you know how much trouble you caused us?" the one bully said.

"You beat me up, so how is that my fault you got in trouble?" I replied, not thinking it would be better if I just kept my mouth shut.

I was immediately shoved into the lockers behind me, while another bully grabbed my back pack from me and threw it down the hallway. The pain in my ribs reminded me of my frail condition.

I stumbled to the floor, and looked around, but being Monday, everyone had deserted the school as quickly as possible. I was on my own.

The beating started from there, but didn't last long. They started to kick me all over, before one of the jerks ripped my facemask off, and chucked it behind him, but we never heard it hit the ground.

The lights in the hallway flickered, and my facemask was tossed back over to me, landing on my chest. The air cooled considerably, a damp wind blowing over us.

"What the hell?" the bully said, as they all turned.

When they saw what was waiting for them, they all went stiff and silent.

There stood my wagon buddy. Almost ten feet tall, cloaked in black, demented smiling mask covering the rotting face behind.

"You boys want to stop picking on my friend?" It asked, each word dripping sorrow.

No response. The bullies were rooted to the floor.

"Nothing to say? Ok, how about I teach you all a lesson your parents refused to teach you?"

"No please," I croaked, putting my shield back on my face.

"Scotty, I appreciate you not wanting this to happen, but if I don't defend you, no one will. Now run along. I will visit later."

I shrugged my shoulders. I knew I wasn't going to convince this thing that it shouldn't cause havoc.

I started to walk away, when I heard movement and

pained noises. Instead of turning, I kept walking, not wishing to see what my friend was doing to my attackers behind me.

I left the school and started to quickly walk away from the grounds, when I spotted my wagon beside a tree, just down the street.

I went over, grabbed the handle and pulled it behind me all the way home.

School was cancelled the next day.

A teacher leaving late that night came across a large pool of blood in the hallway. The boys were each reported missing by their parents, but no bodies were ever found.

My wounds healed, and because there was now several openings on the senior boys' team, I was asked to come play for the rest of the season.

My high school dream had come true. Even better, from playing so many games and practices, I started to tone up, losing some of my pudge. It even caused a few girls to start paying attention to me. Or so I thought.

Emily was the one who I liked the most. She flirted with me, made comments on how tall I was and how big my feet were. I knew exactly what she was trying to allude to, but I was shy and had zero experience with females.

As the school year came to an end, she finally invited me to her place, telling me her parents were out of town.

I should have had my guard up, but being a teenage boy, with the prospect of some alone time with my crush while her parents were gone, was too much for my brain to process, so I went to her place, clearly excited.

Arriving at her place, I knocked, and she opened the door, making small talk. She offered me something to drink, but my head wasn't following too much, I was too nervous at what may happen soon.

After a few minutes, she suggested we head to the basement, as her room was down there. I giddily accepted, and had to stop myself from sprinting ahead of her.

As I descended the steps, I felt my legs growing wobbly. My vision began to blur and I felt fuzzy all over. It wasn't until I made it to the bottom of the steps, and saw that she was standing near some other grade 12 boys, that I realized I had been drugged.

When I woke up sometime later, I could barely

move. My entire body hurt, and I realized that they had beat me senseless again. From the feeling of my face, my nose was more than likely broken again, and from trying to sit up, many of the other bones in my body had suffered the same fate.

I was now only wearing my underwear, and when I finally stood up, I wasn't fully aware of where I even was. My eyes were swollen shut, but I was able to see a little bit out of my left eye, and scanning the area, I wasn't sure where my clothes even were.

I could see I was in a wooded area, and really wished I had at least a shirt, as it was cold. It was day time, the sun was out, but there was still a chill in the air.

I tried to take a few steps, but my feet hurt so bad, I had to sit down almost immediately. That act itself though was also excruciating.

I didn't know how I was ever going to make it home, not even knowing how far away it was. I was in so much pain, I just couldn't fathom taking more than a step.

Then I heard a noise.

Turning my head slowly, I saw my wagon buddy come walking through the trees, pulling my wagon behind it.

"How did you know I was here?" I groaned,

knowing full well my jaw would need to be wired shut shortly.

"Kid, I am always here for you. Some things need to happen, in order for me to act. Hop in, let's go home. You need to see a Doctor, and I need to determine how to respond."

I tried standing up, but the pain was too much. I looked up at the imposing creature, not sure what to do.

"They messed you up really bad. Alright, I am going to pick you up, but do not, and I must insist on this, do not touch any of my skin, ok?"

I gently nodded my understanding.

The creature stooped down, putting one of its arms under my knees, the other behind my back, and then hoisted me up. I was so nervous. Part of me still didn't believe my wagon buddy was a real entity, but as soon as I felt the firmness of its appendages on my body, I knew it was.

Walking over to the wagon, it began to lower me into the wagon, when I cramped up, and I felt my right thumb and index finger touch rotting flesh. The creatures cloak had been pushed up its decaying arm, and inadvertently my hand made contact.

I stared at the eyes behind the mask with shock and fear.

"Oh Scotty. I am so sorry buddy, there is only one

way to keep you alive. Once living flesh touches my flesh, it begins to decay. I can save your life, but there is only one option."

"Please, please," I pleaded. I didn't want to rot!

In one singular movement, my wagon buddy opened its jaws and bit off two of my fingers. I felt the blood drain from my face, and the world went black, my body slumping into the wagon.

I came to sometime later, still in the back of the wagon, the creature slowly pulling me along.

I looked at my hand, only to discover that it wasn't a horrible dream I had experienced, I was in fact, missing two fingers. The lack of blood around the wound puzzled me, but I was still in so much pain, I let that small detail disappear.

"Here we go, Scott, hold on, almost home."

We entered our backyard, and my wagon buddy rolled me up to the basketball hoop. The creature walked over to the house, and knocked hard on the back window, attempting to alert my mother.

The knocking worked. The creature fled into the bushes, as my mother entered the backyard.

Seeing me in the wagon in my current state was too much for her. She let loose a long high scream, dropping to her knees.

The next bit was a blur. An ambulance arrived, and I was whisked away to the hospital and put under for surgery. My level of pain had masked most of the damage I had endured; a broken arm, a broken leg, two of my small toes had been cut off of my left foot, my nose was broken again, four ribs cracked this time, a part of my earlobe was severed, but thankfully it was able to be stitched back on, five cracked and broken teeth, and of course, as I had suspected, my jaw had been broken in three places.

When I woke up in recovery, my mother was sitting in a chair near me weeping.

I tried to speak, but my jaw was wired shut, so it came out muffled and distorted. She understood though, and her head snapped over to me.

"Oh Scotty, I am so, so sorry this happened to you. This is just awful. The Doctor's did great work, but they couldn't save your toes or your fingers. They said if they had the actual missing pieces they could have tried to reattach them, but without them available, they just couldn't save anything there."

I looked at my right hand, saw the bandages, saw the missing area where my two fingers should be, and remembered my wagon buddy biting them off. He saved me, I thought, he came for me, from out of the trees, through the pain, and brought me home. I would forever be indebted to my wagon buddy.

I was heavily sedated for the pain, and thankful for my jaw being wired shut, otherwise I would have spilled the beans on my wagon buddy to my mother. Looking back though, it wouldn't have mattered, she would have believed me to be hallucinating and simply making up a silly story.

"Exactly, a silly story," Detective Linear interjected, startling me. I was so engrossed in telling them what had happened all of these years that I wasn't expecting him to talk.

"Your medical records are clear Scott, your fingers and toes were cut off when the bullies attacked you and left you in the woods."

"That's what my mother told the Doctors. She wouldn't know, nor did she ever know the truth."

"Go on then," the other Detective interjected, clearly frustrated with what he was hearing.

Movement behind the two got my attention, and they both gave each other a sideways glance. Was I hiding something? Being nervous?

In truth, behind my interrogators, I saw movement where I shouldn't have. I knew the one way mirror behind them was for observing my behaviour when I was alone. But now the mirror turned into a window for a slight moment, and standing on the other side was my wagon buddy. Before I could fully digest what I had witnessed, the window returned to a mirror.

"Don't be nervous, Scott, keep going," I was told sarcastically.

When I slowly came down off of my pain killers and was discharged from the hospital, I spent the next few days lounging on our couch in the living room, while I was continually questioned by Detectives, wanting to find out what had happened.

I told them what I knew, and I felt ashamed when I told them the reason I had gone to Emily's was because I was an aroused teenage boy, invited to my crushes home, while her parents were gone. My face flushed, and my mother got up and left the room. I hadn't witnessed her drinking recently, but I knew she still was. She would have went into the kitchen and poured herself a quick drink, not wanting to hear about why I was there.

I told them she invited me downstairs, and when we went down, I felt dizzy and drowsy. I said I remembered seeing the other kids down there, but I was too fuzzy to make out their faces. The next thing I remembered was waking up in the woods in significant pain, stripped down to my underwear.

"How did you get home? We found where you were dumped, Scott. It was twenty miles away from Emily's and thirty miles from your place," the one Detective questioned.

"I don't honestly know sir," I said, "I just shuffled the best I could and slowly made my way back here, before knocking on the window and collapsing into my old wagon."

This seemed to satisfy all of the detectives who came, though none asked why there was no tracks of me walking, but that there were wagon tracks leading all the way back to our house.

As I started to heal up, going to physiotherapy to help with the injuries, I felt anger growing that within a short period of time I had been attacked three times, and ended up with missing toes, missing fingers and permanent scars. And all for what? Because some of my school mates thought I was a loser? I had no father at home? I wasn't a supermodel?

The anger I felt wasn't good, and it made me want to do horrible things to these kids. But at the same time, I knew that they didn't deserve retaliation, because they were clearly going to be prosecuted.

Finally the day came that I was well enough to return to school. I was able to get my face mask removed, and all of my various casts and slings were gone. I was able to walk fairly limp free, but at that time I was very self-conscious of my missing fingers.

My mother came to me on the weekend and asked me if I would prefer to be home schooled for the rest of the year, or if I wished to return. She warned me that I would be seeing my attackers every day, and that they still hadn't been charged with anything, so they may be very angry.

"I think at this point, I need to get back out there. I don't think it's doing me any good to just sit here all day sulking."

"That's a very mature thing to say Scotty," she said, clearly pleased.

So it was decided; on Monday I would return to regular classes. I would be behind in the subjects, but my mother contacted the principal and set up a meeting with her, so that we could discuss things before the day even began.

I didn't sleep well the next few nights waiting for the return to school, but Monday morning came very quickly. We arrived well before the rest of the students would get there and met with the principal. She went over the subjects I had, and we rearranged a few of my courses so that I wouldn't be in class with Emily or any of the other members of the senior boys' basketball team. The only course we couldn't rearrange was physical education, so it was decided that for that class, I would take a spare and head to the library to catch up on course work.

I was feeling relieved after the meeting, and my nerves lowered some. They quickly returned when the morning bell rang, and I remembered I would have to actually go into a classroom.

Entering class number one of the day, the walk in went by in slow motion. I entered the doorway, and all of the students already seated at their desks slowly lifted their heads up to see who it was, expecting the teacher. Instead they were greeted by a 6'3 scared student, who was missing two fingers, who hadn't been attending in several months and who some believed had died.

Eyes went wide, mouths hung agape and I struggled to keep my head up and walk to my desk. When I finally sat down, the teacher entered and welcomed me back. A few people, who were angry I still existed and was bringing trouble to their friends glared at me, but otherwise the morning went by smoothly. I felt lost in most of the classes, being so far behind in the subjects, but deep inside I was feeling so happy to be back in school and not sitting on the couch anymore.

The first moment of the day that really made me feel uncomfortable, came when the lunch bell rang, and I returned to my locker to retrieve my food. Walking there, most of the kids gave me sideways glances, but when I turned the corner in the hallway, I came face to face with Emily and two of the grade 12 boys from the basketball team.

We made eye contact before Emily looked away, but one of the boys wasn't having any of it.

"You loser, do you know how much hurt you are causing people, accusing them of disgusting things."

He then spit on my face, hitting me in the forehead.

I calmly wiped it away with the back of my arm, and then stared straight at him.

"I haven't accused them of anything. The detectives who came and interviewed me over and over are the ones who are forwarding charges. You guys drugged me and maimed me. You will get what's coming to you, but it wasn't because I went to the police, it's because you did this to me."

I pushed through them and walked quickly away, not wanting to get into a shouting match or a shoving match.

The rest of the week was fairly inconsequential. I didn't have any more runs in with any of my attackers, and I started to get caught up with my course work.

Leaving school Friday was a relief.

I went to my locker, got my books together and headed towards the front doors. Half way there, the principal spotted me and waved me over.

"Scott, we need to talk."

I followed her into the nearest empty classroom.

"Scott, an email was reported to us between some students, involving you. It says that you are responsible for the disappearance of the missing students from the basketball team. It also says that you will be held responsible and a credible threat has been made towards you. I have arranged for a police officer to escort you home and we will be in contact with your mother regarding this. Sorry to alarm you, but we felt it was best to get on top of this immediately."

I understood.

It didn't mean I was all too excited to have to go outside in front of the other students, get in a police car, and get dropped off at my house.

Leaving the school, I spotted the patrol cruiser parked near the playground. As I walked towards it, I saw several of the basketball team members watching me, as they hung around their cars.

I ignored them as best as I could, and waved at the Officer. He opened the passenger door, and as soon as I got in, he drove away. He didn't really say anything, just drove, winding in and out of traffic. He was driving faster and faster, and I started to feel a bit worried. I felt uncomfortable with the way he was driving, but didn't want to say anything. I didn't want to question a Police Officer on his driving skills.

I was finally forced to speak up, when he turned

right instead of left, driving away from where my house was.

"Hey, Sir, this is the wrong way," I said, turning to look at him, "I live in the other direction."

"Shut up. Do you know who my brother was? Kyle. One of the boys that disappeared. One of the boys you did something to. Time to pay up Scott."

My eyes went wide, realizing this Officer wanted revenge for something I didn't do. He was speeding up even more, but I knew I needed to get free, and fast. I tried to open the door, not caring that we were still driving, not caring what would happen to me if I jumped out of the moving car. I had been through enough pain recently that I figured it wouldn't be too difficult to deal with some more injuries.

Unfortunately the door was locked, and I wasn't able to unlock it.

"Keep trying buddy boy, that door isn't opening until I say so."

I decided to take a different approach. I decided to be aggressive.

I grabbed the steering wheel with both hands and cranked it.

The car jerked violently sideways, striking a car travelling beside us. As the Officer tried hard to regain control, we were propelled from that impact, across the oncoming lanes of traffic, before hopping the sidewalk, crossing some grass and hitting a light pole directly. This stopped us immediately, deploying the airbags.

My vision was filled with dust and glass, my chest aching from the seatbelt tightening so rigidly, so rapidly. My face was throbbing from the airbag impact, but luckily I didn't think my nose was broken.

Coughing, I looked over to see the Officer releasing his seatbelt. He then proceeded to open his door, walk around the car, and open my door. Grabbing me hard, he started to pull viciously.

"I am still buckled in!" I yelled, being pulled violently, pain flying up through my head.

He leaned over and undid my seatbelt, then pulled me out of the car by my arms, flopping my body onto the sidewalk beside the crushed car.

A few people who witnessed the accident had gathered near us, and the Officer clearly wanted them to leave.

"Back away, this is a violent criminal, get back, everyone get back!"

He was waving for them to leave, but none of them were moving. Finally fed up, he pulled out his gun and began pointing it at people, yelling at them to leave, which they did hastily, what with the threat of death now facing them.

Finally when we were alone, he called someone on his cellphone, talking low enough that I couldn't hear.

It didn't take long until a van pulled up, brakes squealing, and I was tossed into the back. The vehicle took off abruptly, causing me to be thrown against the back doors. When I was able to sit up, I saw that the people in the front, with the Officer, were the other basketball team members, the ones who had been watching me in the parking lot.

Nobody spoke, some watched me, some looked away uncomfortably, but the vehicle sped away.

Finally, we stopped in an old abandoned gravel lot, the doors flew open and the Officer forced me out.

I was still reeling from the impact of the car accident, causing my legs to not fully be under me when I left the van. Taking a few uneasy steps, I stumbled and fell onto the rocks, landing in a puddle.

"Get up you loser. I want to see your face when you die."

I heard the Officer position himself behind me, knowing that if I turned and stood up, he would have his gun trained on my head. I also knew that if I did turn and stand up, he would pull the trigger.

"Hold up," the smaller Detective interjected, "I am having trouble sitting here, listening to your fairy tale, and now I have to listen to you make up tales of this unethical cop? I don't think so. This has gone far enough. Our Officers live and die by the badge, and I won't let you say otherwise."

Detective Linear though, cleared his throat, and then pushed a piece of paper over to his partner.

It was a police report, showing that the Officer had in fact been found guilty of assault, assault with a deadly weapon, kidnapping and attempted murder. It also indicated he was found unable to be sentenced to prison, due to his mental state.

He turned back to me and motioned for me to continue.

So I didn't turn and stand. This angered the Officer and caused some of the kids to start yelling at me. One of them walked over and pushed me down to the ground with his foot, keeping me in the puddle.

"I didn't do anything to anyone! You all assaulted me. You all did this, not me," I pleaded, tears starting to pour from my eyes.

"I promise, please, just let me go, I won't say anything to anyone!" I begged for my life, but again, one of the bullies came over and kicked me hard, shutting me up.

I heard the officer walk up close behind me, and I felt the gun push against the base of my skull.

"Any last words, you useless, fatherless scum?"

I wanted to say something, but nothing would come out of my mouth.

Then a noise from behind all of us got our attention.

"Is that a wagon?"

I heard what the kid said, but I didn't know if I should believe it.

I turned around slowly, still on the ground, rocks grinding into the flesh of my knees and palms. There, near the entrance to the lot, was my wagon, sitting neatly near the perimeter fence.

The kids and the Officer had all slowly walked towards the wagon, not sure why it was there, and wondering what the noise had been. While I was looking, I felt a presence walk up beside me, as the air cooled considerably. I looked up and saw my wagon buddy standing beside me. The creature was looking down at me, mask smiling its crazy wide smile.

"Don't worry Scotty, I'm here."

I was overcome. I started sobbing, which alerted the kidnappers that something was happening behind them.

Turning, they all came to a halt, staring at this new intruder standing beside me.

"Who are you?" The Officer asked.

My wagon buddy didn't reply, instead the creature reached down, grabbed me under my armpit area, and helped me to stand up. I knew my wagon buddy took extra care to make sure I didn't accidentally come into any contact with its rotting flesh.

"Hey bozo, are you deaf? Did you hear my question? I am a Police Officer. You need to listen to my commands. Who are you? I want you away from my perp now. Move nice and slowly, keeping those hands out to your sides."

My friend turned now to face the Officer and the other kids, and I could see them all shrink where they were standing.

"You don't want to know what I really am. But for now, I am your worst nightmare. You all should be ashamed of yourselves. Torturing this innocent lad, all because you believed something to be true, when it wasn't. I am the one who killed the boys, who devoured your brother. Kyle tasted delicious, his fears and regrets satiated my appetite for some time."

When the creature finished talking, it let out a chuckle, the sound of which shook me to my core and caused my arms to break out in goose bumps.

"You killed Kyle?"

The question was meekly spoken, almost in disbelief, as though the Officer couldn't believe what he was hearing.

"I did. Those torturous souls were awful to my friend Scott here, so I taught them the lesson they needed to be taught. Life is harsh and sometimes the consequences of their decisions are also harsh."

The Officer stared at my buddy for a few more seconds before he raised his gun up, pointing it at the creature.

Six quick rapports echoed throughout the abandoned lot, as the Officer fired off the shots. All hit my wagon buddy, four in the face and two in the body. The four that hit its face shattered the smiling mask it was wearing, sending pieces flying.

Everyone stood in stunned silence though, as the creature never moved. The Officer clearly expected it to drop to the ground, its head blown off, but that was not the case.

Instead my wagon buddy reached back into its dark cloak and produced another smiling mask, and covered its face, ensuring I never saw the carnage below.

"That's not possible," a few of the kids said, sounding as though all hope had left them.

"Yet it just happened, didn't it?"

The sarcasm that drenched that sentence from my

wagon buddy actually made me chuckle, and put everyone into motion.

A kid ran towards me, intent on punching me, but never made it. My wagon buddy simply turned, grabbed his arm and pulled it off of his body. The kid screamed in agony, dropping to the gravel beside me, as my wagon buddy began to repeatedly pummel the screaming kid with his own appendage. Once the kid was bashed silent, my wagon buddy swallowed the arm whole, in one gulp, like a sword swallower making a sword disappear into their mouth.

After seeing this a few of the kids turned and began to run away, but my friend wasn't having any of it. It moved fast, as fast as anything I had ever seen before in my life, and appeared to fly through the air, before eviscerating each of the kids as they ran away, leaving their lifeless bodies lying where they were.

The creature then returned to me, just in time to prevent the last, large, grade 12 student, from hitting me with a large rock. Instead my friend drop kicked the kid, sending him flying, before walking over to him, and crushing his head with the rock that was intended for me.

There was only three of us left now; myself, the Officer and my saviour, my wagon buddy.

The creature walked up to the Officer, standing a good 4 feet taller than the uniformed man.

"Kneel," It said to the Officer.

The Officer followed the order promptly.

"Now call it in. Call in what you have done, and when your colleagues arrive, when the Police get here, you will scream from that moment on, until the day you die. You will scream for the rest of time, at the top of your lungs, until your vocal cords are shredded and only a hoarse whisper leaves your mouth."

It didn't take long for the Police to arrive. I was quickly bundled up, and whisked away, my mother and my principal meeting me at the police station. Both of them had been crying and both had been so worried, expecting me to have arrived home hours ago. My principal kept apologizing, saying they didn't know that it was a set up. I didn't blame her, she had truly been trying to help me stay safe.

Life was hectic after this latest event. Interviews with more Detectives, meetings with Lawyers, and more interviews. Finally the trial arrived. Shocking to all in attendance, the Officer who kidnapped me, was found not mentally fit to stand trial. He spent the course of his time screaming at the top of his lungs. He was sentenced to life in the psychiatric care ward at the hospital.

My mother determined the best option for us was to move, so she put the house up for sale, and we moved that summer. She wanted the best life for me, and wanted me to finish high school, so she made what she thought was the best decision.

As for me, I was worried. Ever since my wagon buddy saved me, I hadn't seen them at all. I believed the creature would follow me to our new place, but a part of me was sad, thinking maybe I would never see it again.

"May I get a glass of water?"

My question startled both Detectives, as they were deep in thought, pondering the truth of my words.

"Yes, of course. I believe this may be a good time to pause actually, and have some lunch. Scott, you will need to stay here, of course, but we have a small menu of options. We will bring that back with your water."

"That's awfully kind of you guys, thanks," I said, as the two men left me alone in the room. What I really longed for was to just be able to stand up and stretch. The chair I had been sitting on now for hours was very uncomfortable, and with the handcuffs attached to the table, I wasn't able to stand and stretch at all.

I looked at the one way window, but didn't see anything other than my reflection. I thought for sure when they left my wagon buddy would return.

A very short time later, the two men returned, one

carrying a glass of water, as well as a full pitcher of water, and the other had a laminated piece of paper.

"Hey Scott, here is your water, and I brought a full pitcher so that you can just refill as needed. My partner here has the menu. Once you are done eating we will continue."

"Thanks guys, that's very nice of you. Is there any way possible that I could maybe stand up? Just to stretch even?"

The two men looked at each other, before Detective Linear produced a set of keys. Selecting a small key, he unlocked the handcuffs from the table.

"Why don't you decide on what you want to eat Scott, and we can go for a walk to the washroom. Then we can come back, you can eat and we will continue."

That sounded like a great plan. A part of me though was wondering if this was all a ploy. They suddenly had decided to become nice to me, for no other reason than being nice? They clearly were trying to get me to open up with the hopes of me suddenly confessing that my story was made up and that I was in fact the murderer. This of course, wasn't true, and I wasn't about to confess to anything.

The walk felt amazing. I didn't even care that I was in handcuffs. Just to stretch and move my limbs was a relief.

After eating, the men asked if I needed anything else before continuing.

"I'm good to keep going, if you are?"

They both nodded they were good to go.

So I continued.

My mother moved me to a small town, about ten hours away from my old school. Rumours of how I lost my fingers and how I got my scars started immediately, but I wasn't bullied for them, or made fun of. I was instead turned into a student with an air of mystery surrounding him.

I was able to play basketball again, but our team wasn't good and we didn't really travel for games.

I ended up graduating, and enrolled in a community college, deciding I had a love for teaching, but wanted to stay near to my mother.

College was great, I devoted myself to my studies, and for the first time I was around a diverse group of free-thinkers. Being around such eclectic people boosted my confidence and I was less self-conscious about my scars and missing fingers.

I developed my first true group of friends and on weekends I even began to socialize, something I had never done before. I was truly awkward at first, but soon fell into a rhythm, and I couldn't help but feel that I had found what I had been missing for so many years.

Unfortunately that meant I neglected to remain in contact with my mother as much as I had promised. She would call and leave messages for me, and I didn't mean to not contact her back, but time slipped away, and before I knew it, I hadn't spoken with my mother in almost two months.

When I called her finally, early that Saturday morning, I knew she wasn't doing so well.

"Hey, so sorry I haven't gotten back to you sooner, school has been crazy. How are you doing? I will be home soon for the Christmas break."

I could barely understand her reply. She was slurring her words so badly that it was hard to even guess at what she was saying.

"Mother, sorry, I can't follow what you are saying. How much have you had to drink?"

She erupted back at me in response, but again, I couldn't understand her or piece together her words.

"Ok, you know what. Call me back when you are not so drunk, and when I can understand you."

With that I hung up the phone, feeling instant regret at doing so.

I pushed it away though. For too long my mother

had been drunk while I had needed her. So I went about my days as normal, waiting for her to call.

She finally did the following weekend. She apologized over and over, promising to stop drinking, and excitedly discussed my coming home for the semester break.

It was a great conversation and we left it off on a good note. I would be home after the semester for two weeks, and I was looking forward to some downtime from my studies.

I had almost completely forgotten about my wagon buddy. The creature though, hadn't forgotten about me.

Now, I had also neglected to tell my mother that I wouldn't be returning home for the holidays alone. I had met and fallen madly in love with Megan. We had met in class, became study buddies, good friends and finally boyfriend and girlfriend. She didn't care about my scars, missing fingers or toes, or the fact that she was my first girlfriend. She said I was everything she needed; funny, sweet, kind and caring. She also liked how my hair was longer and I was taller. I was guarded at first, remembering how my "romance" with Emily had turned out, but eventually I relaxed and we began having a great time.

When the semester finally ended, I was so excited to have her spend the holidays with us. Her parents had decided to go to Mexico for the winter break, and Megan couldn't afford to go, so I invited her to join us. She was more than happy to accept. She however, thought I had told my mother she was coming.

The entire drive to my small town, to my mother's place, I was a wreck.

Finally about twenty minutes from arriving, I confessed to Megan that I had not told my mother that she was coming, as I wanted to spend time with both of them, and I didn't want my mother to feel put out.

"Oh Scotty," she said sadly, "you really should have. She might be very angry. Maybe even disappointed that she isn't having you all to herself."

"I know, I was just worried that she would say no."

I turned down our street, and pulled up beside the house, glad to see that my mother's car was parked in the driveway.

"Tell you what Megan, I will go in and tell her you are here, and we can go from there."

She agreed that this was a good plan, so I jumped out and jogged up to the front door, frightened for my life.

Knocking on the door, I hoped it would take a bit for my mother to come to it, but much to my chagrin she opened it almost immediately.

"SCOTTY!" she yelled, throwing herself onto me in a large hug.

"Hey, great to see you," I replied, returning the hug.

"Come in, come in! Boy I am happy to see you," she enthusiastically chattered.

She stopped walking when she realized I hadn't entered the house.

"Mother, I should have told you, but…. I brought a friend with me. I brought my girlfriend, Megan."

She looked stunned. She stared at me blankly. Finally her mouth broke into a small smile.

"Well, that's just great kiddo. I am so happy for you. Bring her in, the three of us will be here for the holidays."

My mother disappeared into the kitchen, so I ran back out to retrieve Megan.

"How did she take it?" Megan asked when I got to the car.

"Pretend happy, I think, it was hard to tell."

I grabbed our suitcases and we went inside.

My mother was sitting in the kitchen, drinking straight from the bottle. It appeared to be vodka, but as I didn't drink, I wasn't too sure.

"Are you ok mother? I'm sorry I didn't tell you Megan was coming."

"It's fine Scotty, its fine. All the men in my life leave me for a younger woman eventually right? I guess I am just not worth anything to anyone."

She threw back another big swig, and kept on talking, voice already beginning to slur.

Megan just stood behind me, clearly uncomfortable, but also wanting to be near me, to support me.

"Mother, it's not like that at all. You will always be my mother, Megan may one day be my wife, but there is always room for you in my life, and in our life."

My mother slowly turned and looked at me, at us. She stood up and walked to the sink, and ran the water for no reason for a few seconds. She then turned and before I could process her actions, threw the bottle of alcohol at me as hard as she could. I tried to duck, but wasn't fast enough, and it caught me square in the chin, blood bursting forward, pain flying through my jaw.

"What the hell!" I bellowed, grabbing my face. My mother stormed by, pushing me out of the way, and appeared for a moment as though she was going to push Megan too. She wasn't having any of that, though, and she stepped back, away from her as she marched by.

We heard my mother grab her car keys, and leave the house, slamming the door behind her. The car started outside, and the engine revved, as the vehicle drove away quickly.

"Should we go after her Scott? She shouldn't be driving. She's had a lot to drink it appears."

"Nope. It's too bad. That was so uncalled for. I think I might need stitches. Can you take a look?"

Megan looked and sure enough she thought it would be best for us to go to the small local hospital and get it looked after.

"Yeah, we see your medical records here for your chin, Scott," a Detective chimes in.

"Yup, eight stitches to close the wound," I reply. Not knowing what he was trying to allude to with his comment.

"So while you got your chin stitched up, first responders were trying to cut your mother free of her car?"

I slowly nodded. Yes they were.

I was at the hospital getting stitched up, when a police officer came and asked to speak with the doctor.

The Doctor listened to what he said, then came back over to Megan and me.

"Listen Scott, I am just going to finish this last suture here, then I am going to escort you down to the OR. Your mother was in a pretty severe car accident. To be upfront with you, it doesn't look good. So sit still and we will get moving."

I never saw my mother alive again.

That night, Megan and I were sitting in my mother's house, on our old couch, trying to make sense of what had happened. Would this not have happened if I had just told my mother Megan was coming?

Was I to blame for this?

Megan told me I wasn't, but I couldn't help but feel responsible. My mother needed to stop drinking, and clearly when she told me she wasn't, this had been a lie. But if I had prepared her that Megan was coming, then maybe she would have been able to mentally process the information first, maybe even cut back on her alcohol intake.

"I just need some air," I said, "let me go for a quick walk, and I will be back. Feel free to have a shower, or see what food is in the fridge, but I just need to take a few minutes on my own."

Megan understood, and said she was going to go have a shower while I went for a walk.

I went out into the cold December air, glad for my thick jacket and my snow boots. The sun had set, and the moon was bright, guiding me on this walk. I wasn't sure where I was going to walk to, but I started anyways, putting some distance between me and the house.

I thought about all the fun times my mother and I had together. I thought about how she worked hard to support me on her own, how she tried to be a father figure to me when needed, and how excited she had been for me when I went off to school.

"My son, going to school to be a teacher," she would say frequently, beaming with pride.

I also thought of all the times I had wished she had been a better mother. All the nights she was passed out on the couch while I ate dinner. All of the school occasions she simply missed; parent-teacher meetings, school plays, and special theme days.

Now it was just me. No mother, no father, just me, Scott, all by himself. Except I wasn't.

A noise off to the side startled me, and when I looked over, I was surprised to see a community basketball court. It was closed for the winter, the nets removed from the hoops and the court covered in snow, but there it was. Standing beside the closest hoop was my wagon buddy, who waved excitedly when I looked over.

"Hey Scotty! Hey man, come over here! Boy have I missed you!"

I walked over to see the creature, realizing it had been years since we had last spoken. Not since the abandoned gravel lot.

"I thought you were gone?" I asked, not meaning to sound hurt, but it came out like that.

"I never left."

I was wearing a thick jacket and gloves, meaning I was covered up pretty well, no skin exposed. That came in handy as I fell into my wagon buddies arms, hugging the creature tightly.

I sobbed hard. This was my only family now, this creature. This abomination had always been there for me, and now here it was, when I needed it again.

After I calmed down, I released my hug, and stepped back.

"Thank you, I needed that."

The creature's mask was always smiling, but now behind it, I could see the rotting flesh of its cheeks curl up, it smiling as well behind the mask.

"You are welcome. It is great to see you Scott. It's been too long. I am proud of what you have been up to. College is a big deal. You are setting yourself up for success in the future. If only those bullies could see you know?"

"I'm lost right now," I said, "I'm not sure how to move on from this?"

"Scotty, this will sound awful to hear, but your mother didn't have much time left on this earth. She was dying Scott. She hadn't told you yet, but she had an aggressive cancer. Only a few months left to live, by what the Doctor's said, and by what I could foresee. What she did to you was unacceptable, and had to be dealt with."

I stood stunned. Was my wagon buddy saying that it was responsible for my mother's death?

"I know what you are thinking Scott, but no, I had no part in the accident. That was your mother's drunken state and the poor conditions of the road. Other forces were involved in that, I am afraid to say. But she harmed you, and the universe responded. Now return to the house, enjoy your time with Megan, and I will visit you again shortly. Things are coming towards you Scott, handle them appropriately, and remember, I will always be here for you."

With that my wagon buddy walked away from me, disappearing behind some bushes.

I returned to the house, trying to decipher what my friend had meant, but not having any luck.

"Is this where you tell us how your 'friend' killed Megan?"

Every time the Detectives talked, it startled me. Hearing their voices, they sounded so foreign, as though they were calling me long distance and the line had a poor connection.

"When was Megan killed?" I countered, before continuing on, annoyed at the latest interruption.

Life was a struggle over the next five years. Both Megan and I managed to finish college, and both of us were hired as teachers. Sadly we were hired at separate schools, but the commute was only twenty minutes from our place for both of us, and so we made it work. We had long days, long weeks and long years, and in our 3rd year of being teachers, we found out that Megan was expecting.

This was amazing news. We had both discussed having children for some time, and now that it was about to become a reality was phenomenal.

But as always, darkness stayed on my periphery. Five months into the pregnancy and no heart beat was detected.

The hurt of losing the child was too much and it caused Megan and me to grow apart. I drifted away, began drinking beer, for the first time in my life, and Megan went elsewhere, into the arms of one of her colleagues. I was beside myself with anger. This was Megan doing to me what my father had done to my mother.

But being hurt is being hurt. While I was devastated we had lost the child, I hadn't been the one carrying it, and I understood Megan needed something more. I wasn't supplying the companionship she needed anymore.

She moved out, and moved in with the new guy, and I stayed, and got drunk and missed work.

One day, a few months later, I was disciplined for time missed, and put on a probationary leave. I was livid. This was Megan's fault.

That night I had seven or eight drinks and then got in my car and drove to Megan's new residence.

I yelled and I cursed and I stomped my feet in their yard.

Finally the new guy came out, and instead of telling me to go home, or that he was calling the police on me, he walked straight up to me and sucker punched me straight in the nose, dropping me where I stood.

"You come here again Scott and I will kill you," he said, standing over me. I was flopping around on the ground, disoriented and trying to get my bearings.

"Who are you?" I heard him say, and looked towards him.

My wagon buddy walked up, slowly, calmly, and reached out, grabbing the guy around the neck, lifting him up off of the ground.

"Scott is in a bad place right now, you are part of

the reason. I will spare her, slightly, but she will be punished as well."

Then the creature squeezed and the guy's head popped off. From my position on the ground, it looked like something straight out of a cartoon.

Megan came running out from the house screaming, seeing her new guy's head on the ground, his body slumped beside it and I crouched on the snow.

She ran up to my wagon buddy, ready to attack, but came to a screeching halt, when it spoke.

"Quiet, move no more. You will stay away from all involved from here on out. You will not go crazy, but you will cry and scream if you think of me ever again."

Megan lived the rest of her life in seclusion, which is why most people think she is dead.

"May one of you fill up my glass with some water please?"

One of the Detectives reached slowly over, filled my glass and put the pitcher back onto the table.

"Why don't we have a report on this dead guy? There is no mention anywhere of Megan's new significant other being killed?"

"Not sure," I replied, and I truly wasn't.

"Carry on then, some of us want to go home

tonight. Some of us are able to go home tonight," he said with a snicker.

It took me some time to straighten my life out after that. I had loved Megan so much, and to lose her completely was devastating. But then, to also have my wagon buddy make it so that she would never come back was even tougher. The creature had been my one and only true friend, for pretty much my entire life. So I knew I would have to forgive my wagon buddy. It was just going to take some time.

I joined a program to stop drinking, and found a newfound joy in running. I took to it with great enthusiasm, and managed to become pretty proficient, even though I was missing some toes.

On one of these runs, late one night, I came across an old playground, and I wasn't surprised to see my wagon buddy swinging on the swings. It had been about two years since I had last saw it, while it was destroying Megan's partner.

"Hey," I shouted, leaving the road and jogging towards the swings.

"Hey right back stranger," it replied, jumping lightly off the swings, and walking towards me.

We stopped, facing each other, about three feet apart.

"Hey Scott. I'm really sorry for what I did. I didn't mean to cause you so much pain. I just wanted to protect you and in doing so, I stole Megan from your life. I know you probably won't be able to forgive me, but I just wanted to say, if you do ever need me, you know I am here for you."

The creature turned and walked back slowly to the swings, hopping back on, and started pumping its legs, getting the swing moving.

"You know what," I replied, "I did hate you. You ruined any chance of Megan coming back to me. But who knows, maybe it's for the best? We became two different people. I want to say I do forgive you. You have always been my friend, and other than my students I have now, I am all alone. My mother and father are both gone, and I don't even know if he is even alive. You are the only constant I have, and while I have no idea what you even are, I know you truly care for me. I just want to say, I am glad you are in my life, and I am thankful for your friendship. I also want to say, you need to visit more often. Two years is too long to not see you."

My wagon buddy chuckled, continuing to swing, getting higher and higher.

"Thank you Scott, that means the world to me. And

yes, two years is too long. I wasn't sure how long you would need, how much time you needed to come to terms with what I did."

I nodded my head in understanding.

"Now before I go Scotty, I have a question for you."

The creature kicked hard, the swing pumping higher and higher. I thought for sure it would do a complete circle around the frame that it was attached too.

"If you want to know what I am, I can tell you. I can fill you in and teach you about how I came to be, the place I am from and why I was chosen for you. All you have to do is ask."

I had never thought of this possibility. At first my wagon buddy was just simply my imaginary friend. Clearly it had evolved since then.

"Thank you for your offer. That means a lot that you would be willing to share. For right now though, I don't want to know. Right now, I just want you to be my friend."

"I accept that reply Scott. In the future you may ask. For now, I will leave you be to finish your run. I will see you soon."

The swing went up, and when it came back down, the creature wasn't on the swing anymore. It rattled and clanged without any body weight on it.

I jogged back home, happy to have my friend again,

slightly curious as to what its answers would have been, if I had asked.

My wagon buddy was true to its word, and the creature would come around and visit every second or third day. It was great, and it even prompted me to move out of my condo and buy a house. I made sure the house had a secluded back yard, and I was able to put in a brand new basketball hoop.

The first night my buddy visited me, seeing the hoop set up, I could tell how excited it was.

"Just like old times," it said as it appeared out of the shadows.

"You were so small back then Scotty, but you were braver than you ever gave yourself credit for. You never were scared of me, and you should know, I am one of the most frightening creatures in all of the galaxies."

I bounced the ball to the creature and watched as it casually dunked the ball, cloak flowing behind it.

"So what's next for Scott? You have a plan for the future?"

"No, not really. Maybe train enough to run a marathon? Maybe get a dog. You ok with a dog?"

"Oh yeah, dogs love me, and I can pet them and they won't die, so that's always a nice bonus. To feel love under your fingers, and not worry about that love withering and dying, that's divine."

Just two friends, passing time, waxing philosophically while shooting hoops. If someone walked by and heard us, they would have no idea it was a man and his imaginary friend turned death dealer.

Thinking back, I am glad I never got a dog. They are lots of work; feeding, walking, and cleaning up after them. I was gone so much running and working, it wouldn't have been fair.

I probably never would have reconnected with Emily either.

"Wait, you reconnected with the girl responsible for your beating, loss of toes, and subsequent kidnapping?"

Detective Linear sounded flabbergasted.

"What can I say? She was my first true crush, she was gorgeous then and was gorgeous years later. She found me, so I went with it."

I was grocery shopping one day when a voice behind me spoke my name.

"Scott, sorry is that you Scott?"

I turned and I was stunned to see Emily standing there.

"Emily? Wow, I never expected to see you again. Or more specifically, I never expected to speak to you again."

We turned the small talk into a coffee get together. From there it became dinner.

Over dinner, I found out she was never charged with anything, and it took her some years to see that she had helped instigate and it wasn't my fault.

She had been married briefly, but was cheated on and he left her. I was glad to find out it wasn't any one of the kids from the basketball team.

We caught up on life and our careers, and I was pleased to hear she was working as an elementary school teacher across town. She laughed when I said I was teaching middle school, as only another teacher laughs.

We left that night with plans to meet up again the next weekend for dinner and a movie. She kissed my cheek and walked away into the night.

I was on cloud nine Monday morning, even if it meant returning to work. My fellow teacher Mike noticed and asked why I was in such a good mood. I filled him in on reuniting with Emily, but left out the torture and kidnapping from my youth.

"Emily you say. From over at Hawthorne? Interesting."

The way he said it was strange, but I was too elated

to read anything into it. I left for the classroom, excited for the weekend to return.

When Thursday rolled around, Mike stopped me in the staff room, and motioned for me to join him, away from everyone else.

"Ok, listen Scott, we have never really been friends too much, just said hello and such, but when you mentioned Emily, that name rang a bell. I talked to my friend over at Hawthorne. If it is the same Emily, I hate to break it too you, but she is married. She has been married for 10 years to the same guy, he teaches PE over there, and I guess he used to be a basketball player at one time."

I heard what he was saying but didn't want to believe any of it.

She told me she wasn't married?

"Ok, thanks Mike, I'm so confused right now. I will just talk to her at dinner on Saturday and see what's going on."

I had a sinking feeling in my stomach. I thought she had changed. This felt like a set up all over again.

I let Friday come and go, never really mentally there. I was floating, numb, trying to decide what to do.

Finally, later in the day, I decided I would just call her when I got home.

She beat me too it. When I got home, I had a message on my machine from her.

"Hey Scott, sorry to call so late, hey something has come up and I can't make dinner tomorrow night. Did you want to do lunch? We could even have lunch here at my place if you liked. Otherwise would dinner Sunday work? Call me back, I am fine with anything really."

I called back and wasn't expecting her to answer, but on the second ring, she did.

"Hey Emily, sorry I missed your call. Hey, would Sunday dinner here work? No? Ok, did you want to do it at your place? Yes, ok that sounds great. Shall I bring anything? Are you sure? Ok, so what time works? 6 works great. Alright, see you Sunday at 6."

Quick, to the point, and fairly emotionless.

Late that night, I heard a basketball being bounced outside. I went down and wasn't surprised to find my wagon buddy playing some hoops on its own.

"Hey Scotty! Sorry did I wake you?"

"Yeah, that's ok though, I was having trouble sleeping."

"It's a set up. Don't worry though. I have your back. You won't be waking up in the woods this time."

The creature bounced the ball to me, then walked away, disappearing into the darkness.

Sunday night came, and I brought a fairly cheap bottle of wine.

Emily acted delighted, but I didn't really care.

Knowing she was married and that it was a setup, had me angry and on edge. I was a bit snappy to some of her meaningless questions, but after a glass of wine, I simmered and we began having a good time chatting.

While we talked, I kept scanning the room, looking for signs of a husband. It appeared that many photos had been taken off the walls or simply flipped down. The first time Emily went to use the washroom, I dashed over to a flipped down picture frame. Turning it over, I was a bit annoyed to find a photo of a dog, not a photo of her and her husband.

Emily returned and I boldly asked her about the flipped down photos.

"I had to cancel our dinner last night because my dog became really ill during the week and I had to put him down. I haven't had the heart to move his photos so I just flipped them down, or in some cases took them off the wall completely," she said, pointing at the blank spots that indicated missing pictures.

"Oh, I am so sorry to hear that Emily, I was worried that the pictures had photos of you and your husband," I blurted out. As soon as the sentence left my lips, it caused Emily to spit out her mouthful of wine all over me.

"Oh god, I am so sorry, here let me get some paper towel," she yelled as she hurried to the kitchen, and came back with some sheets.

"You didn't say no," I coldly responded, as we both dabbed wine off of my face and shirt.

"I didn't know it was an actual question," she replied, "but I am glad you have been enjoying your wine."

I knew right when she said those words, that she had set me up again. She had poured the glasses, and she had once again laced my drink with something. This time is was a lower dose, designed to hit me later, making sure my guard was down.

I felt fuzzy, dizzy and drowsy.

"Scott, you actually think I wanted anything to do with you. God you are still such a loser. This time, we are going to make sure you don't have legs to walk back to town with. You created so many issues for us for so long. You deserve what's coming to you. What you don't deserve is to ever have your body found."

As she finished speaking, I lost full control of my legs and fell off of the bar stool I had been sitting on. I hit the ground hard, but didn't lose consciousness. Emily came over, and stood directly above me, smiling as though she had just won the lottery.

Another person walked beside her, and I kind of recognized him, as being a grown up version of one of the students on the basketball team.

"Drag him out back," he said, "we will cut his legs off first out there."

I felt somebody else grab my arms, and then I was sliding on the floor, unable to do anything to be stopped.

Emily opened the double doors, leading out to the back patio, and I felt the coldness of the deck wood on my back as we left the house.

I was dragged off the patio, and I saw that they had stopped by a basketball hoop.

"Tie him up to the pole, someone get the extension cord, I am going to get my saw. The faster his legs are off the better I am going to feel," the man I kind of recognized said.

Emily looked at me and saw that I was laying there with a wide smile on my face.

She kicked me hard in my side, clearly perturbed that I was grinning.

"Why are you smiling?" she said, while winding up and kicking me again.

"You think I caused all of this. You guys brought this on yourself. I wish you had been smarter Emily, it's too bad you are going to die because of your stupidity."

She kicked me square in the mouth, bursting my lip, but thankfully it didn't feel like she had broken any teeth.

The person returned with the extension cord, and I head the saw get plugged into it and turned on. The scraping sound of the blade starting sent chills down my drugged spine. I had to have faith though. My wagon buddy would be here, the creature said it would be.

"Ok, hold him down. There's going to be a lot of blood, but we all need to stay strong and power through this. Once this loser is dead and gone, we can put our troubles behind us. Why is he smiling?"

The guy I kind of recognized was staring at me now, thrown off by my wide grin.

"He says we are going to die," Emily said, sounding uneasy.

"How? He's doped up and being held down. We have a saw. How are we going to die?"

Then I heard a familiar noise and felt a familiar cooling of the air.

I turned my head, and my smile grew wider.

My old wagon came slowly rolling into the back yard.

"Hey guys, what's the meaning of this?"

Everyone jumped when my wagon buddy spoke. They all turned, seeing the large creature sitting on a patio chair on the deck.

"What the hell are you?" Emily called out.

"Exactly," my friend replied.

They all appeared confused, looking from one to the other. I, on the other hand, began to laugh. I was pretty doped up, but I knew that they were at the end of the line, and nothing could save them now.

My wagon buddy moved swiftly. Maybe it was my drug influenced state, or maybe the creature did it for my benefit, but I watched my friend move at warp speed, while the adults appeared to move in slow motion. First the creature grabbed the saw from the hands of the male adult, and used it to cut him in half, body segments falling away, one part to the left, one part to the right. Then the creature grabbed the other male, and appeared to swallow him whole. My buddy was facing away from me, but I saw it take its mask off, and its head expand, before it picked up the human and dropped it into its mouth. Then the human was gone.

Quickly the hell spawn grabbed who I presumed was Emily's husband. It had replaced its mask onto its now normal sized head. It broke the man's right arm above the elbow, then did the same to the left, the man screaming in pain. The creature then repeated the process on his legs, both above the knees this time. With the man now writhing in pain on the ground, my wagon buddy simply jumped high into the air, before landing directly on his skull, crushing it like a watermelon, dropped from incredible height.

Only Emily remained. I was still too groggy to stand up, but I was trying. Pulling myself over to the patio, I was trying to use the wooden beams to hoist myself up, but wasn't having any luck.

"Scotty. What shall I do with this female? She has caused you immeasurable pain. Shall I do the same, to her?"

I was still chuckling, but the question burned into my brain, beyond the drugged haze.

"You know what, I don't want to cause her pain. She clearly has issues. So I think I am going to be the bigger man, today, even considering what she has done. So good buddy, you do what you see fit, but I am staying out of it."

I felt great saying the words. I knew the creature was going to do something horrendous to the wench, but I wanted to stand above that, I wanted to be the better person, and I knew I was. This was years of pain and suffering, but also years of planning and tracking me down. All for what?

I finally got myself standing, the drug starting to wear off. They had slow dosed me, thinking that by now I would have been cut up into numerous pieces.

"I am going to go in and have a drink of water, then we can go home. Do what you will."

I slowly shuffled into the house, tripping and stumbling over the door jam, before making it over to the sink.

Running the water, I heard Emily scream behind

me, a noise I would never forget, but one I knew meant that this chapter in my life would be over.

I heard footsteps behind me, and turned to see my wagon buddy enter the house.

"Let's go Scott. You are in no condition to drive. I will pull you home and come and get the car."

"Sounds good. Thanks buddy, I really appreciate you saving me again."

The creature came over, and patted me on the shoulder.

"You know it friend."

We walked out to the wagon, and I slumped into it.

Then the creature started pulling me, walking faster, then jogging, before running.

When I woke up it was sunny out, and I knew it was morning. I knew my headache would settle down with some Advil, and some food. I looked outside and saw my car in the driveway, causing me to smile.

"Yeah, yeah, great tale. You know we have never found any evidence of this 'slaughter'. Good story, but let's get to the lady in the wagon from Saturday night. The one with you on video."

Both men were visibly annoyed, shifting around, frustrated to still be here.

"Well I am finally there, apologies, but you said to tell it again."

Behind them, once again, I caught movement. This time I wasn't as obvious about looking, not wanting to draw any extra attention again. I glanced at the bigger detective, but I looked beyond him. He clearly thought I was making eye contact, when in fact, I wasn't focused on him at all.

The glass shifted again, and standing in the observation room, looking dark and gloomy as always, was my wagon buddy. The smiling mask was prominent, the cloak pulled up high. I wanted to wave, but I knew my friend would be joining us soon enough, and I didn't want to have to tell the Detectives why I was waving.

"Carry on then, but hurry up, the day is growing long."

I nodded, and continued.

I decided it was best to move on, to start over once again. I took a job in a neighbouring town, working in a warehouse; shipping and receiving. When I interviewed for the position, I was told I was over qualified and the work would be beneath me, but I explained that I had suffered a loss recently in the family and I just wanted steady, quiet work, where I would come in, put my head down and grind. I didn't want to spend time with the public or the public's kids and just needed a breather. I also said it was a perfect job, start early, end early and I wouldn't have to move. I loved my house and loved my backyard basketball court.

By this time my wagon buddy and I had developed a fairly fierce rivalry. Whether it was 3 point shooting contests, 1-on-1 games, or just playing HORSE, neither of us wanted to lose. I suspected the creature let up on me sometimes. It did have a height advantage as well as magical powers at times.

Either way, I had isolated myself. It was just me and my buddy, and I worked by myself.

It didn't take long before I began to neglect some things and unfortunately someone called the city bylaw officers on me.

"You mean this report?"

A piece of paper was pushed across the table, and glancing at it quickly, I nodded that it was the complaint.

The bylaw officer who knocked on my door wasn't who I was expecting. I was expecting the pizza delivery guy, so when I saw a younger, attractive lady at my door, I was a bit thrown off.

"City Bylaw. We have had multiple complaints regarding cleanliness, garbage disposal, yard care and odor. Are you the owner of this property?"

She was straight to the point. If I had known it was bylaw when the doorbell rang, I wouldn't have answered.

"Yeah, I am. I'm sorry, my job is pretty strenuous and the hours are long. It makes it difficult for me to get to everything. The garbage has to be out by a certain time, and if I put it out too early it gets knocked over and goes everywhere. I have tried, I just haven't done a good enough job. I am so sorry."

I was trying to be smooth and get a warning, but it was not to be.

"Everyone has excuses, everyone either gets it done, or is fined, evicted or jailed. I don't care what happens as long as you clean it up and let people enjoy their neighbourhood. As of this visit, you have 60 days to bring it up to city standards. I will visit again in the next few weeks and if I see no progress, I may expedite that time line and make it easier to repossess the land and get the legal side rolling. Your call. Consider this being served."

With that she handed me a city citation document and made me sign a form.

She was gone before I even knew what hit me.

"Scott, this isn't good. She will come over whenever she wants."

My wagon buddy actually startled me when it spoke. I didn't expect it to have entered the house. In fact, I was certain that was the first time it had ever entered my house. Normally we just stayed outside. It had entered Emily's house to take me home, but never, in all our years had we spent time inside.

"I know," I sighed, knowing I had to get my butt in gear, "I will get it handled."

I worked long hours, and when I got home I put in more long hours, trying to bring the property up to the Officers standards. I didn't realize how much junk had accumulated and how much I had let the grass grow. The entire place was out of control and over grown. Except the basketball area. I always made sure that was useable.

With about two weeks to go until the deadline, I thought I was good and finished. The front yard was landscaped nicely, I had disposed of all of the garbage, and had trimmed the trees in the backyard. The place was looking brand new, which made the visit from the Bylaw Officer that much more frustrating.

It was about eight o'clock at night, and I had

already crawled into bed, having to get up at four the next morning for work. A loud pounding began outside, and I realized it was someone knocking aggressively on the front door.

I went out to see what was going on, and was surprised to find the bylaw officer at the front door, flanked by six Police Officers.

"Surprise inspection!" she shouted before the officers proceeded to start looking around the property.

I wasn't even angry, I was annoyed. I wanted to be sleeping, not standing here dealing with this person.

"I don't think a surprise inspection is really necessary. I have went above and beyond what you asked for. Can you hurry up please, I would like to go back to bed. Work comes early."

I heard some banging and crashing behind the house, and decided I wasn't going to let anyone wreck any of my stuff. I left the front deck, ignoring the Bylaw Officer telling me to stay where I was.

Rounding the corner, two Police Officers were tossing garbage everywhere. This wasn't my garbage, this was something they had brought with them. I was furious when I saw this.

"What the hell are you doing? Why are you throwing garbage around my backyard?"

"Hey Jan, we found garbage everywhere here," the one Officer yelled out to the Bylaw Officer.

"You want to ticket him or arrest him?"

"How about neither," I said, temperature boiling, "you did this to my yard. How about you clean this up and get off my property?"

"Are you causing an issue here? Are you going to resist arrest?"

I was close to losing it now. Arrest? Resisting? How could I resist if I wasn't under arrest?

"So now I am under arrest? For you guys dumping garbage in my yard?"

"No one is under arrest Scott," Jan the Bylaw Officer said, "what I need you to do is have this place compliant by this Saturday. Otherwise you will be evicted by city enforcement."

I was so confused. I was confused by what she said, confused by the Officers dumping garbage in my yard and confused when they left as quickly as they had arrived.

I was even more confused by why I was still being targeted.

I spent the next few days ensuring the yard was completely cleaned. I disposed of the garbage the Officers dumped and made sure that I had raked the grass clippings as well. I took a video of the place, with the time and date, showing what it looked like, to protect myself from this corrupt Bylaw Officer and waited for her arrival.

I waited. I waited and waited as Saturday kept going by, slowly, hour after hour.

My frustration grew. I was told that today would be the inspection date, and now here I was, waiting for the Bylaw Officer to come, and still nothing.

I went into the house and called the bylaw office. I was told I was scheduled today, but they couldn't guarantee a time.

"I have been here, all day, waiting. I have rights too you know," I blustered, trying not to yell at the person on the phone.

They understood but that was the best they could do.

It was getting close to 5pm and I decided it was time to eat some dinner, having missed lunch. I microwaved a few frozen dinners and ate them, watching the news, annoyed at losing an entire day.

After finishing dinner, I went out back to see if my wagon buddy would be up for some basketball. There was no sign of the creature.

"I thought you would be around?" I questioned, grabbing the ball and beginning to shoot.

A voice from the shadows replied.

"I don't think it's safe for me to be out here with you right now Scott. The bylaw enforcement could show up at any time."

I nodded, understanding.

I focused on shooting some longer range shots, and after hitting 1ten in a row, missed the 11th when a ladies voice startled me mid-release.

"Surprise," the Bylaw Officer said.

After grabbing the ball, I was a bit confused to see it was just her.

"Where's the rest of the patrol?" I sarcastically questioned.

"I gotta say Scott, you actually got this place cleaned up. Too bad it won't matter. I am here to evict you."

"WHAT!" I yelled, turning and throwing the basketball hard against the wall of the house. I was furious.

"How can I be...?" I started to say, but when I turned to face the Bylaw Officer, she was facing me, pointing a gun at my head.

"What's the meaning of this?" I asked, a lump in my throat.

"I didn't think you would recognize me. We never talked, but you saw me in court. Only I was younger. You took my brothers from me. Kyle has never been found. And my other brother, you got him put away for a long time. He was a good cop, Scott. I know he didn't kidnap you. And now he just sits in a padded room, making noise. He used to scream all day long, but now his voice has been destroyed. It's because of you Scott, and now you will pay."

I shook my head in disbelief.

"Look, I get you are angry, but this is NOT MY FAULT! He kidnapped me, falsely I might add. Kyle attacked me, the kids attacked me, I DON'T GET WHY I KEEP GETTING BEAT UP AND TREATED LIKE THIS FOR SOMETHING THAT IS NOT MY FAULT!!"

I turned and started walking away, but she wasn't having any of that. A warning shot rang out, causing me to drop to the ground. The bullet went by, hitting the wall of the house.

"Don't you walk away from me you piece of garbage," she growled.

I turned, facing her, almost wishing she would pull the trigger. This absurdity needed to come to an end, and maybe it would, with the sound of a gunshot.

"Look, Jan was it? I am really sorry you feel so hurt. I was assaulted, beat up, and sent to the hospital. Then I was drugged, tortured and had my fingers and toes removed. Following that, I was kidnapped, beat up and had a cop, your brother, dump me in a gravel pit, where a gun was put to the back of my head. I was then lied to, drugged again, and had someone attempt to use a saw to cut my body parts off. And to top it all off, all of this is apparently my fault, because those kids thought I was a loser for not having a father at home, and for looking dumb. I have had one friend my whole life. I have no family. So you know what, go ahead and shoot me. But you better act fast, because trust me, you don't want to meet my friend."

The lady looked a bit unsure, after I had finished talking, but she didn't lower the gun that was pointing at me.

"You don't have any friends Scott, you are a loser, and you are going to die."

"No, I don't think he is," the voice boomed from the darkness.

My wagon buddy walked out of the gloom, mask on, still after all of these years unsettling me.

"Who are you?" she asked, voice trembling.

"You wouldn't want to know who I really am. But for posterity's sake, I am Scott's friend. You know the one who he doesn't have, according to you. I am also your worst nightmare. Scott won't be dying tonight, but you will be. This will be the end of Scott's troubles, from you, from your family. He will be free of this constant harassment. Now, how would you like to die? Quick or slow?"

Jan moved the gun from me to my friend and squeezed the trigger four times, hitting the creature in the chest four times.

"You will need to do better than that," it said, before walking towards her.

She fired off one more shot, as it got near, blowing its mask off its face.

Then my friend pounced on her, ripping her throat open with its mouth. I could hear a deep sucking and slurping noise, as the creature drained her body of all of its blood.

When it was done, it set her gently in the wagon. It grabbed another mask from within its cloak, and placed it on its face, before turning to face me. The creature was always cognizant of ensuring I didn't see what was beneath.

"People have heard the gun fire Scott, you need to take this wagon to the swamp near here, and dump the body."

I knew this was both a bad idea but also a time sensitive idea. I also knew that my friend wouldn't steer me wrong.

I grabbed the handle and quickly walked around the house, heading down the sidewalk, staying away from the Bylaw Officer's vehicle.

Detective Linear tapped the table between us, tapping his fingers on the folder with the photos.

"This is when you were caught on her dash cam, as you went by."

"Yes that's right, and my wagon buddy followed behind, briefly as you can see."

He shook his head in annoyance.

"Scott, I can agree that there is something weird behind you guys, but for all I know, it's a reflection from your television, or a long left over Halloween decoration. I don't know, it's something, but I don't think it's a 9 foot tall boogeyman."

His partner chuckled at the boogeyman quip.

"Carry on," he said, clearly exasperated with my story.

I went quickly down the road, turned and followed the pathway over to the edge of the swamp. I dumped her body, by just tipping the wagon over, making sure not to touch her. Then I took my wagon and rushed back to the house, worried about what to do with her vehicle.

When I got back, her vehicle was gone, and there was no sign of my wagon buddy.

Then about a week later, you guys showed up and arrested me.

So here I am. I guess I am guilty of a few things; aiding, hindering investigations etc., but I have never once murdered someone, that's a fact.

So now, here we are.

"Yes, here we are. You know we don't believe a single word you have said right? There is no creature. Actually, back that up. There is a creature, but the creature isn't make believe. The creature is you, Scott. You are a monster, and you are the murderer of at least 5 people, if not more. We will find their remains, soon enough, and we will link you to all of it."

I shook my head no, I was telling the truth. Behind them again, the window went from one way glass to a two way window and I could see my wagon buddy standing there. The creature made a slicing motion across its neck as though a knife blade was being used to cut it open. It then pointed at the two men. I knew what it was implying. Should it take them both out?

The two men looked defeated, clearly wondering how to get me to confess. Unfortunately for them, there would be no confession. They wouldn't be leaving this room.

"Hey buddy," I called out, jolting both of them from their thoughts, making them look at me. They saw I wasn't looking at them, but beyond them, looking at the glass behind them.

"Go ahead," I said, "make it quick, I can't handle

this anymore. Maybe of these days, someone will believe me. Until then, let's go home."

"Who are you talking to?" Detective Linear asked.

"He is talking to me," the voice boomed behind them in the room.

My wagon buddy was now leaning against the corner of the room, behind the two Detectives. Its cloak was black, it wore the ever smiling mask, and it looked casual with its position.

"Who the hell are you?" they both asked, fear crossing their faces.

"Exactly. Why I am Scott's wagon buddy. You know, the one who doesn't exist. Scott isn't responsible for any of the deaths you asked about. I killed each and every one of them, and they all deserved it. Now Scott has said for me to finish you both off. This may not be the best option for Scott and his future though."

"How did you get in here? You killed the people? You are under arrest," the other Detective yelled, drawing his gun from his holster, while Detective Linear stepped closer to me.

"I am under no such thing. Now, if you let him leave, I will let you two live. You wipe the books of him and any trace of Scott being here. You will never again bother him about any of this. Understand? The other option is for you both to die. What shall it be?"

Detective Linear looked quickly at me, and saw that I was smiling.

"He's telling the truth, we should just let him go."

"No way Linear," the other detective said, and took a step towards the intruder.

"Ok, last warning gentlemen, I would love to let you live, but I am also very hungry. Is Scott leaving or is he staying?"

"We need to let him go, now," Linear said, sounding stressed and panicked.

"Nope, not happening. I am going to give you this last command. I am counting to 3. If you are not on the ground with your hands behind your back by 3, I am going to open fire. Understand? 1....2....3," He slowly counted. My wagon buddy didn't move.

When he got to three and the commands hadn't been followed, the Detective cracked off three quick rounds, two striking the chest of the invader, one striking the mask.

My wagon buddy didn't flinch.

Instead, it lowered its face, so that we couldn't see its face, pulled a new mask from its cloak and put it on.

"What the hell! I just shot this guy three times Linear!"

"It's not a human," Linear replied, "We need to let Scott go!"

After shooting my friend three times, I knew even if

they let me go, they weren't leaving this place alive.

"Scott, I need to get you out of here, and fast. Others will have heard those shots and will be coming soon. Turn your head, please, I don't want you to see my true face."

I understood. Sometimes what has been seen, can't be unseen.

I turned away, making sure I wouldn't see anything in the reflection of the observation window either.

I heard wind, something moving quickly, and muffled squeals.

"Ok," my friend said, and when I turned my head back, the two Detectives were gone. Their guns and badges were sitting on the table in front of me.

"Here's the keys, you will need to unlock the cuffs, and I don't want to touch your skin."

Of course I thought, and unlocked the cuffs, releasing my wrists, rubbing the skin where they had been digging in.

We left quickly, and I wasn't sure how we would leave unnoticed. My wagon buddy must have been using some of its powers, as we walked out of the building without a single sideways glance.

Waiting outside at the curb was my wagon.

This brought a smile to my face.

"Jump in!" I yelled, "It's my turn to take you for a ride!"

My wagon buddy plopped in, and immediately I felt all of its weight disappear.

"Run, Scotty! I want to feel the wind blowing through my mask!"

"Run all the way home, let's go play some basketball!"

So I grabbed the handle and ran.

It was just me and my wagon buddy, and I was free.

Without my friend, I would be completely alone. I never had any real friends growing up, but the creature was always there for me. I didn't have a father, but this thing taught me lessons in life, that I never would have learned otherwise. My mother tried her best, but now she was gone.

I didn't know what the future held. I had confidence the police would leave me alone, but I also knew at some time in the future, my friend would need to feed again.

I would be there for it when that happened. That's what friends were for, after all.

That's how my small part will end for now. Just a man and his friend, feeling the wind blowing across his face, and through the mask of the creature.

We both had smiles on our faces, and an extra one on its mask.

END

AUTHORS AFTER NOTE

Ah Wagon Buddy! Love this story. Another one of my longer stories, much like Yuri.

It was inspired by a Bonfire Night picture I saw of a little girl pulling someone in a wagon with a Guy Fawkes mask on. The image was just striking, and I started thinking about what could be happening with the backstory. I am by no means a good crime writer, but wanted to write a supernatural crime story, and this is what happened.

This story was originally going to be included in my Left Hand Path short story book, but after seeing the length, most people that gave me feedback indicated that they would like to see it as its own release, and I don't think I could agree more!

Big thanks to Mason McDonald for this amazing

cover! He also did the cover for Yuri and Left Hand Path, and it has been greatly appreciated!

Big thanks to J.Z. Foster for all of his help behind the scenes. If you are not reading his stuff, seriously go get it, great writer, better human!

Massive huge thanks to David for editing this beast. (Still if you find anything it's on me.)

Big thanks to Justin M. Woodward as well for help behind the scenes! Read his stuff!

If you liked this or if you hated this, please leave a review! It helps us big time!

The world of being an indie author is a hard path, with how much stuff we tackle, but it is worth every single thing we do and word we write!

So thank you to every single person who has read my stuff!

Find me at;
Stevestredauthor.wordpress.com
Facebook.com/stevestredauthor
Instagram.com/stevestred
Twitter.com.stevestred
stevestred@gmail.com

Until we meet again friends!

Steve

ABOUT THE AUTHOR

Steve Stred is an up-and-coming horror author. He has several releases out already, including; Invisible, Frostbitten: 12 Hymns of Misery, Left Hand Path: 13 More Tales of Black Magick, as well as the novellas Jane: the 816 Chronicles and Yuri.

Outside of writing, Steve works as a Certified Canadian Pedorthist.
When not working, he enjoys spending time with his wife, son and dog!

Steve is based in Edmonton, AB, Canada.

ALSO BY STEVE STRED

Also From Steve Stred:

Short Story:

- Gabe & The A Word (2017)
- Auryn Meets the Dragon (2017)
- Layne Meets Lefty & Knuckles (2018)
- Gabe and Layne: The Battle to Save the Playground (2018)
- Ayrielle and Willow Band Together! (2018)

Full Length:

- Invisible (2017)
- Frostbitten: 12 Hymns of Misery (2018)
- Left Hand Path: 13 More Tales of Black Magick (2018)

Novella:

- Jane: The 816 Chronicles (2018)
- Yuri (2018)
- Wagon Buddy (2018)

FREE PREVIEW

Please enjoy this free preview of my novella

Jane: the 816 Chronicles

What would you do, if hope was your only option?

JANE PART 1

Jane

Jane knew the drill.

The doctor came in. The door would close, loudly locking behind them.

The doctor, wearing the lab coat, the gum boots, the big, thick rubber gloves.

The doctor, wearing the biohazard face mask, head draped in white with the clear plastic window, eyes peering out at Jane.

Jane stood in the corner. Slowly, her sad, hurt eyes, would lower from the doctor's face, down the doctor's chest, along the doctor's arm, to the end of the doctor's hand, where always, the drill was clenched. Every time, when Jane finally made her way to the hand, she would notice the slight tremor. The drill would be shaking ever so slightly.

Jane, would then make her way back to the doctor's face, hoping, pleading, that she would see kindness and sympathy in the doctor's eyes. Every time, though, she saw fear, disgust, and perversion.

Penny knew the drill.

Like clockwork, every day, she would hear the door slam shut, in the room next to hers. Jane's room.

She would hear the doctor shuffle in, know Jane was in the corner, and would wait to hear the tool start, and then would slowly slink to the floor in the far corner in her room, her cage, and cover her ear holes. She would cover them up, as tight as she could, with the long skinny fingers of her hand, trying to block out the sounds of that instrument. Trying, desperately, to block out the sounds of Jane's pleading, crying, begging and ultimately screaming.

Jane, always wishing for sympathy, always hoping today was the day, that the doctor stepped aside and opened the door, letting her leave, felt a tear leave her desperate eyes, and make its way down her scarred cheek, towards her stitched together mouth.

The doctor took two steps towards her, mumbling for Jane to stay still, and grabbed Jane's grotesquely long arm. With the other hand, the doctor turned on the drill and pushed the drill bit into Jane's checkered forearm, immediately drawing a black, thick liquid, or what Jane had grown to learn, was her modified blood.

The pain began to sear through all of Jane's being. She tried to hold her scream in, she wanted to show she was brave and strong, but her nervous system was over rode, and the sound began deep in her elongated throat. Before she could fight to keep her lips clenched together, the scream flew out. Immediately the doctor stopped the instrument, back handing Jane hard across the face. The brilliant shock and pain, snapped the scream right out of Jane's throat, and caused her to stumble backwards a bit.

"QUIET YOU FREAK!" the doctor howled at her, turning the drill back on, pouncing onto Jane again, reinserting the drill bit into her brutalized forearm.

Penny, heard a different noise this time. She had never heard the doctor yell before. Never heard such hurtful words towards one of them.

When the instrument started again, Penny heard a new noise. A noise closer to her.

She looked over, at the entrance to her cell, and saw a set of eyes gazing at her, through a sliding window in the door. She had never before seen this sliding window, her room was 4 cement walls, with no windows at all. And when the door was closed and locked tight, sealed from the outside, it was almost impossible for her to find the door frame. At times, she would think, she was in the far corner from the door, only for it to open, and she would in fact be sitting beside it. Her cage could be very disorienting.

The eyes stared at her. Dark. Cold. Uninviting.

Penny's saucer shaped eyes, stared back. Like Jane's, they were also sad in nature, but gleamed with hope. When the eyes blinked, and she saw malice behind the lens now, she knew this was not her rescuer.

Should she speak? She was still sitting on the floor in the corner, scabbed knees, pulled up high to her concaved chest, long arms wrapped around them, hands covering her ear holes. What if she spoke and this new set of eyes was attached to a doctor? And this doctor came in with a saw instead of a drill?

The doctor turned the drill off, pulled it out of Jane's arm, and wiped more of the black sludge off the drill bit, into a vial. The doctor took out a black sharpie, made some annotations on the vial, before returning both the vial and the sharpie to their lab coat. The doctor went and knocked on the door, but as it was unlocked and began to open, the doctor turned and walked back towards Jane. As Jane raised her hairless head up, to the see what was happening, the doctor back handed her again across her face, making her piece work nose start to gush thick, black fluid.

"DO NOT SCREAM LIKE THAT AGAIN, YOU MONSTER, OR ELSE."

With that the doctor turned, leaving the room, the door swinging shut behind them, and the bolt locking firmly.

Penny, now felt the door close over on Jane's side. Slowly removing her hands from her ears, she glanced back at the door, but the sliding window had closed and Penny once again, could not make out where the window had even been.

Moving quickly and fluidly, Penny went to the corner, to the wall that was shared with Jane's cell, and arriving, stood to her full height and raised her right arm fully, until it touched the ceiling. She slowly began tapping the top of the cage, waiting to hear Jane reply.

Jane, still had tears flowing from her eyes. Her forearm was still oozing, her nose had clotted a bit, but felt slimy, and her heart felt like it was going to slow to a stop and explode with pain. She wasn't a monster or a freak. She was their creation. How was as this her fault? Suddenly she felt a reverberation, her head twitched up and her senses picked up a noise in the corner. PENNY!

Penny was tapping for her. Jane, sensing this, quickly and fluidly moved to the corner, pressing her full height up against the wall. Raising her left hand, she felt Penny's warmth radiate through the concrete, and started tapping the ceiling across from Penny. It took approximately 10 seconds of synchronized, rhythmical tapping, before they entered each other's thought stream. There, in the subconscious trance, Penny ran over and gave Jane a hug. Jane began to cry, as Penny kissed her tortured cheek and rubbed her pock-marked back, letting her hand flow over all of Jane's deep scars.

Jane was fully sobbing now. Penny was whispering *"I know dear, I know, but one day soon, we will be free."*

The sliding window opened on both Jane and Penny's doors at the same time. The two workers stared in through the windows, small video recorders in hand, documenting this new event they had discovered.

In each cell, the blue-purple skinned, 9 foot tall bodies, were pressed firmly against the walls, 2 feet of concrete separating them, each with one hand outstretched and rhythmically tapping, a dull hum emanating from each of their purple lips.

Penny slowly stroked Jane, trying to get her test tube twin calmed and centered, knowing that lately the torture inflicted on Jane, was too much for her to mentally take, that this latest verbal attack, on top of the physical torment, would be a tough one for her.

As Penny consoled her, she felt a prickle along her narrow, cratered spine. Something or someone, had entered her cage in the real world.

The scientist, entered the room. The specimen, 815, known verbally as "Penny", was still pressed against the cold wall. As the scientist approached, they slowly unfolded the collapsible wand-Taser, quickly flipping the switch to "On", and pressed the trigger with their finger, swinging it through the air. As the Taser approached 815's side, the scientist noted the specimen tense up, and at the last second, attempt to move out of the way. 815 though, was in the corner of the room, and was unable to move to its left, causing it to hit the wall firmly, allowing the wand to make full contact along its side, and down its right thigh. It yelled out in terror and shock, and lashed out towards the scientist, 815's full 9 foot frame engulfing the surprised investigator, knocking them to the ground. At that same moment, two armed guards stormed into the room, and began to pummel 815 with two blunt sticks, making contact with 815's head.

As Penny was smashed in the head, her long muscular fingers continued to dig into the invaders face, drawing fluid. She felt her subconscious connection with Jane break, and felt herself begin to lose her own hold on consciousness. As she fell to the floor of her cage, she lunged towards the open door. The last thing Penny saw, before going fully black, was the outside of her cell. Floor upon floor with the same layout existed, beyond the door of her jail cell. She made out cell after cell, stacked side to side and on top of each other, as far as her eyes could see. And she could see figures in white lab coats, military fatigues and biohazard outfits. And finally she saw one door open, with a figure in fatigues standing at the opening, shooting a giant blast of flame, into the opening. She could hear the screams of the inmate pierce her brain, as she finally lost her battle, and closed her eyes.

As Jane felt Penny be ripped away from their safe place, she too was struck with an object. Feeling black viscous fluid drip down her neck, she turned and hurled herself, towards her own intruder. As her 9 foot frame flew through the air, she had a moment of regret, as instead of the standard doctor standing there, covered in plastic and lab coat, a beautiful woman of about 30, stood at the door way. Wearing a white blouse, knee length, form fitting skirt and high heels, Jane realized she had never seen anything so beautiful. As she let up in the air, and landed short of her intended target, the lady reached out and stroked Jane's head, wiping away the fluid with a white cloth in her hand.

"Tie her up," the lady said gently, and immediately two military soldiers restrained Jane's arms, and wrapped zap straps tightly around her wrists. Throwing her to the ground, they did the same to her ankles. Once fully restrained, the lady took two steps towards Jane, heels clicking on the cement floor.

"She got too close, disgusting freak, you guys need to be faster," she said, voice now changing from the gently tones, to a gruff anger. With that she brought her right leg back, and then kicked Jane as hard as she could in her face. Wincing at the pain, the lady clicked out of the cell, as Jane started weeping, laying on the floor.

Penny came too slowly. She remembered what had happened, and what she had seen and heard, but she didn't know for sure, just how long ago that was. Was it minutes? Hours? Days? Everything was so groggy and fuzzy.

She knew she wasn't restrained, but now realized she was sitting in a chair. A light clicked on, near to her face, and she slowly opened her eyes, having trouble adjusting to the light.

Penny heard an instrument start up, different than the drill, and then felt a soft hand, touch her arm.

"Hello 815. I am your creator," a ladies voice softly spoke to her, "and I am here to see what you are made of."

As she spoke the last soft word, Penny felt one of

her fingers get wrenched into an awkward angle, and blinding pain begin, as the finger was cut into with the saw. Her eyes adjusted to the light immediately, and Penny could see her left, little finger leave her hand. She screamed in horror and in agony, as the black fluid now spurted from the hole, where her finger used to be.

"Hmm, still black and thick," the lady said out loud, although it seemed she said it more to herself, than to anyone in particular.

Even as Penny was writhing in pain, a doctor in a white lab coat came over, took the detached finger from the soldier who had cut it off, and started to stitch it back onto Penny's hand. Once they were finished, Penny's creator took a closer look, and seeming to be in approval, nodded, and left the room. Just as the door started to lock, it reopened and the lady walked back in, quickly, and went straight to Penny.

"815. I will be honest with you. I like you. You have done well with all of the tests and experiments we have done. You haven't once fought us, until today, and you haven't screamed like 816 has. Overall, you are very low maintenance. I believe you deserve a reward. Will you walk with your creator?"

Penny was in shock. Her hand still burned with unending, deep pain, her eyes still leaked tears, but her heart filled with joy and hope once again. Her creator wanted to reward her. The most beautiful person Penny had ever seen, wanted to spend time with her? She excitedly nodded her head, yes, yes she said, unable to verbalize an answer.

"Come then, 815, your destiny awaits."

The creator held out her hand, and Penny took it, and stood up, leaving the chair. Penny, or 815, was 3 feet taller than the creator, even with her wearing heels, and had to stoop to leave the room she was in.

Outside the room, Penny found they were in a long dark hallway. Looking to the far end, she could see a light, and her and her creator began walking to it.

"You see 815," the creator began," my time is short. I have been here far too long, and I need to transfer my being, to a new host."

They had reached the end of the hallway, and as the creator pushed the door open, Penny was once again shocked, to see how bright the next room was. It was filled with clear walls, and white tables. Long, skinny bodies were laid on the tables, each with a black plastic sheet draped over them, not long enough to cover their feet. Most were purple, stitched together and blistered.

"815, I apologize for my deception, your reward was for you to walk to this room. But ultimately, after the numerous tests we have performed, you will not be a suitable host."

With that, four guards grabbed Penny, and dragged her to the floor. Zap strapping her arms and legs, they dragged her across the floor, as she screamed and attempted to free herself. The soldiers pushed through another door, into a room filled with stainless steel tables, and trays and trays of medical instruments. The soldiers then violently hoisted Penny onto the nearest table, quickly releasing her limbs, only to buckle them down again with the belts attached to the table. The creator walked in, grabbing a long scalpel, from amongst the assortment of surgical tools, already on the tray.

Before Penny could process what was happening, the creator walked to the head of the table and slowly slid the scalpel across Penny's neck. Black liquid began to pour from her neck, and she started to gasp for air. Choking on the fluid now, Penny began to grow dizzy, her eyes filling with water. The creator brought a clear, large vial over to Penny's neck, allowing a good portion of the fluid to fill up the vial.

"Sorry 815, you just didn't meet my expectations, no matter how low maintenance" she said, as she downed all of the fluid in one swig.

The last thing 815, Penny, ever experienced, was the darkness of the black plastic sheet pulled over her face, and she felt the coldness, as her feet remaining exposed.

Jane came too, laying on a cold slab of metal.

The room was illuminated with a far brighter light, than what she had in her cell.

"Hello 816," the pretty lady said. "816, I am your creator. Your subconscious friend, 815, is no more. I slit her throat minutes ago. Now I need you to speak, I need you to say a word to me, or I will slit your throat as well." As she spoke, she slowly pulled the scalpel, held in her hand, across the stainless steel counter top, making a slight humming noise.

Jane's eyes flew open in fear and sadness. Penny was dead. Jane felt the deepest sorrow in her transplanted heart. She yelled a garbled noise. She screamed a pained scream. But no words were articulated.

The creator walked over slowly, unbuckling Jane's arms and legs.

"Stand," she directed, and Jane slowly stood up, stretching out her immense frame. Her head throbbed from where the creator had kicked her face, and her body ached from the beating.

"Walk," the creator directed again, and immediately Jane bent at the hips, her hands hitting the ground, and with her legs straight and her arms straight, she began to move forward, see-sawing her limbs back and forth.

"NO!" the creator loudly yelled. "NO, NO, NO, NO, NO!"

The creator slammed her other hand down hard on the stainless steel table, shocking Jane, and rattling some of the instruments in the tray beside the table.

"Do not ever amble like a dog, do not sway back and forth" the creator barked at Jane, "walk like me or find your time short in my presence."

Jane straightened back up. It made no sense to her. How was she to move forward like the creator?

Gently, Jane placed one long leg out in front of her, and shifted her torso on to it. Then she repeated with the other leg. Soon she was moving forward, balanced, like the creator, who noticed the rapid progress.

"YES, YES, YES!" she gasped, "Now speak!"

Jane pursed her lips together and pushed air through it. An unrecognizable sound came forward. She was determined to impress the creator. She knew that if she could will herself to take some forward steps, she could will herself to speak, to make words. She didn't want to die like her beloved Penny.

"Maaaahhhhhhh," she voiced.

The creator took two tentative steps over to Jane, and gently stroked her arm. She lovingly looked up into Jane's eyes, noting how the right one was blue, the left was completely black, with no white at all.

"Yes dear, you can do it," the creator softly said to her.

"Maaaahhhmmm," Jane voiced.

"What did you say?" the creator asked in revulsion.

"Mom?" Jane replied.

The creator pushed Jane hard away from her, and swung in her direction, slicing Jane across the face with the scalpel, barely missing Jane's throat.

"NO! I AM NOT YOUR MOTHER, I AM YOUR CREATOR YOU ABJECT FAILURE, YOU ABOMINATION!"

Jane pulled her long body to the corner, quivering in fear. She brought one long arm up, covering the side of her face, and stared back in disgust at the creator. Why was she being so mean to Jane? Why would she call her such hurtful names and cause such pain?

Jane could now feel the thick black fluid flow over her patched together chin. The scalpel had cut her deep, and as she touched the side of her cheek, she could feel the flap of skin hanging loose, away from her face.

"GET OVER HERE NOW!" the creator bellowed at Jane. Jane, slowly started to get up to obey the order, but as her legs began to straighten, the creator lunged towards her, arm outstretched in front of her, scalpel wielded to strike.

Jane felt something she had never experienced before. Anger. Deep, burning anger. It rose up from underneath her love of the creator, the hope in her heart, and the fear in her eyes, to overtake her head and cause her to snarl and lash out. Jane struck the creator with her right arm, and gouged the creator's side with her left foot. The creator fumbled the scalpel, and fell backwards, slamming into the stainless steel instrument tray, directly behind her.

"YOU DARE STRIKE ME?" the creator roared, half in shock, half in sad question.

Jane froze in place. She felt an answer form on her lips.

"Y-e-e-e-s-s-s-s-s," she stuttered out. At the reply, the creator smiled. A genuine, warm, loving smile. The creator knew, 816 was her future.

Jane saw the love in the smile, the warmth in the creator's eyes, and she stood up fully, 9 feet tall, and extended her arms in a gesture that the creator immediately understood.

Jane was extended her arms to hug the creator.

The creator took two steps towards Jane, dropping the scalpel, and extended her arms as well. Jane enveloped the creator in her long, skinny, sinewy arms, and squeezed her tight. The creator wrapped her arms around Jane's patchwork back, and Jane thought, this isn't so different from when Penny would console her in their subconscious meeting place.

As Jane kept hugging, she began to feel a warmth deep in her heart. Love. Love, for the creator, love for the new sensation of real, emotional, physical contact. The warmth of the love began to grow, cascading into a hot heat. Jane could feel her arms sizzling and her torso burning. She smiled wide, eyes closed, and squeezed harder.

The creator also felt the warmth. At first she was intrigued. Was this some sort of unknown photosynthesis power, which 816 had developed? Was she able to use other contact from a human, and manipulate that touch to warm herself? But as the warmth became heat, and the heat became unbearably hot, the creator realized 816 was burning her alive. She began to scream as her skin fried and blistered, and she shrieked in horror as her face began to melt, then dissolve and become part of 816 permanently.

As the creator dissolved into 816, the door to the stainless steel room was flung open, with two military personnel entering, both brandishing machine guns. 816 released her hug, which was now just her, having her own arms wrapped around her torso, and stood fully upright, turning to face the two figures.

Jane had no fear in her heart and no pain left in

her head. The creator had not only dissolved into Jane's body, but Jane felt like the creator's mind had transferred over to her own, through some type of acid osmosis.

Jane had memories and thoughts and ideas, none of which were her own. She could see the creator's plan, and what was to come. And 816 could see how she would escape this prison.

The two military figures trained their weapons on 816. 816 still standing, facing them, not moving at all.

"HALT, DO NOT MOVE 816, WE ARE GOING TO RESTRAIN YOU!" one of the figures barked at her.

816 wasn't having any of that. She felt her mind enter both of the figures subconscious at the same time, and smiling her grotesque, black fluid filled, smile, had them turn their assault rifles on each other. Both fought Jane's intrusion, both trying desperately to not squeeze the trigger, but Jane's mental strength, aided now by the creator, overwhelmed them, and with a series of loud reports, both figures lay dead in the room, peppered with gunshot wounds.

Jane, still upright, sauntered out of the room, immediately pushing through an exit door, which she was initially unaware of, when the creator and she had first walked down the hallway, towards the light.

This door, led her back to the cell block she had been imprisoned on, since she was big enough to leave the incubator she was grown in. Above and below her, military personnel were in the process of destroying all of the other remaining numbers, whether by flame, by gun, or by gas. Everywhere Jane looked, as far as her eyes could travel, the cells were being opened and the specimens that the creator had developed, were being eradicated.

"STOP!" Jane yelled in her head, and immediately all movement ceased.

"JUMP!" she yelled again in her head, and like lemmings, every military individual walked to the railing, in the middle of the giant compound, and hurled themselves over the edge. As bodies rained down around her, Jane made her way to the only entrance, which led in or out of the prison complex.

At the door, 816 noticed a digital panel on the wall. Replicating the creator's voice, allowed the thick, concrete door to slide open, exposing the wilderness beyond.

For the last time, 816 looked back. Bodies were still falling from the levels above.

Specimen after Specimen stood at the railings, looking at her with hope and love. Thankful that she had saved them all.

816 waved back at them, and they all replied with a wave of their own.

"JUMP!" she yelled in her head to them as well,

and they all began to hurl themselves over the railing as well.

Jane turned and walked through the compound door, stooping down, so as to not bang her head, and exited the compound, smelling the clean, wild air, ahead of her.

As the door closed behind her, Jane smiled widely.

She was free.

She would always miss her friend Penny, but she was free.

Dropping down onto all fours, legs and arms straight, torso bent, as she used was used to moving, she see sawed back and forth, away from the compound, towards the tree line ahead.

She was still smiling.

She had hope in her eyes.

END

Copyright © 2018 by Steve Stred. All rights reserved. No part of this book may be reproduced in any form or by any electronic or mechanical means, including information storage and retrieval systems, without written permission from the author, except for the use of brief quotations in a book review. This is a work of fiction. Names, characters, places, and incidents are a product of the author's imagination. Locales and public names are sometimes used for atmospheric purposes. Any resemblance to actual people, living or dead, or to businesses, companies, events, institutions, or locales is completely coincidental. Wagon Buddy by Steve Stred – 1st edition.

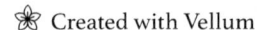

❀ Created with Vellum

Made in the USA
San Bernardino, CA
29 September 2018